FEARED BY HELL

FEARED BY HELL

THE UNBELIEVABLE MR. BROWNSTONE™ BOOK ONE

MICHAEL ANDERLE

DISRUPTIVE IMAGINATION®

FEARED BY HELL

Special Thanks
to Mike Ross
for BBQ Consulting
Jessie Rae's BBQ - Las Vegas, NV

Thanks to the JIT Readers

James Caplan
Sarah Weir
Peter Manis
Kelly O'Donnell
John Ashmore
Kelly Bowerman
Joshua Ahles
Tim Bischoff
Kim Boyer
Micky Cocker
Larry Omans
Edward M. Rosenfeld
Veronica Torres

If I've missed anyone, please let me know!

Editor
Lynne Stiegler

To Family, Friends and
Those Who Love
to Read.
May We All Enjoy Grace
to Live the Life We Are
Called.

A lison sighed as she walked down the street, then looked down toward the cracks under her feet and chuckled at herself. She couldn't believe she was going through with this.

She pulled her jean jacket tighter around her to fight off the light breeze. She shivered, unsure whether it was from the weather or concern over her plan for the day. Meeting two strange men who'd been referred to her over the internet didn't strike her as her brightest idea.

Bright or not, it was unfortunately the only lead she had.

The creepy dude from the internet forum swore up and down that if anyone had gone missing in the area, she needed to contact Denji and Naoko Ishida.

As far as she was concerned, internet forums didn't provide the safest information very often. Or, well, *ever*, really, but she didn't have any reason to think he was setting her up. It wasn't like she'd told the guy on the internet she was a fifteen-year-old girl.

She wasn't a *complete* idiot.

Thanks, Dad. I don't know what you did to Mom, but you better hope I never catch you.

A red flare in the distance caught her attention. Alison tilted her head in its direction.

Pain. Fear.

Something yelped nearby and she rushed toward the sound, her heart beating hard.

Her trip brought her to a wide drain pipe. Something whimpered in the blackness inside.

Okay, I could reach in there, but what if it's some sort of shape-shifting clown kid-eater from the other world that snuck over? Can't trust anything, not with all the magic stuff going on.

At least that was what the more useful tidbits gleaned from the internet had taught her.

Alison sighed and shook her head. The red emotional flare couldn't be easily faked, since that would require someone to know about her abilities. She reached down the drainpipe and gritted her teeth, hoping nothing would bite her and she wouldn't encounter slime.

A wet tongue licked her hand. She gasped, then laughed as she leaned in farther. A quick tug later, she'd pulled out one poor scared dog.

The dog started licking her face, and she giggled and tried to dodge the anxious ministrations.

"You're welcome, boy." Alison's hand traced his collar until she found a tag. "And you're not a stray." She ran her fingers across the raised letters on the metal tag to figure out who the dog belonged to.

"*Annnnnddd* here's your owner."

The Ishida brothers could wait. A scared dog needed his person.

James rolled up the street in his black Ford F-350 extended-cab. Its gleaming paint could have convinced some people the vehicle was brand new, and not just a well-maintained classic, but he didn't give a shit either way. He took care of his truck because it took care of him.

Plus, older vehicles were better. They had less crap to hack.

The last thing he wanted to deal with was chasing a bounty only to find out the asshole had used some extender drone to get into his truck and fuck with his brakes.

Which would goddamned suck.

James grunted. If it wasn't fucking gadgets, it was stupid magic—always something to kill you or make your life even more inconvenient. That was why he kept to the philosophy of KISS (*Keep It Simple Stupid*).

Not a lot of ways to screw up punching or stabbing a guy.

Sure, sometimes you had no choice, but when you did, picking something complicated would fuck you almost every time.

Crazy magic artifacts or fancy tech could backfire, blow up, or otherwise make your day—or month for that matter —a total fucking hell.

He spotted a lithe teen girl in a thin jean jacket standing on the sidewalk, a black lab sitting beside her.

Not just any dog… *His* dog Leeroy.

James slowed his truck and looked around for drones. The lack of drones didn't prove it wasn't an ambush, but it cut down on the chance that someone was spying on him. Most of the human criminals had gotten lazy and relied too much on tech—at least those who couldn't get their hands on Oriceran artifacts or freelance magic practitioners.

Confident he wasn't going to get shot up, James pulled the truck flush with the curb and rolled down his window.

"Are you James Brownstone?" the girl asked, staring at him.

"Yeah," he affirmed, his voice low and deep. "And that's my dog."

She gestured toward a nearby drain pipe. "He got trapped in there."

James looked at the pipe and then back to the girl. "And you got him out?"

The girl nodded. "I wasn't going to let him just stay stuck in there." She stroked his neck. "Poor guy was terrified."

James opened his door and stepped down, or, more accurately, hopped down. The high tires paid for themselves when he needed to go over rough terrain, even if it made a few things more inconvenient.

Leeroy wagged his tail and barked, James opened the back door and patted the seat. The dog tore away from Alison and leapt into the back.

She laughed. "I guess he *is* your dog. Or he's just stupid." She wiped her jacket off.

"Both." James slammed the door. "Thanks, kid. You got an account? I can transfer you some money as a reward."

He looked her up and down, trying to judge her age and taking note of the little streaks of dirt Leeroy must have gotten on her.

Kids might as well be some weird-ass monsters from another world. He could never tell if they were ten or sixteen. Her dark hair ended in white tips.

He figured that was more a teenage thing.

"My name's Alison Anderson," the girl told him. She bit her lip and sighed. "I don't need money."

James shrugged. "Suit yourself."

"I do want something, though."

He let out a chuckle. People always did.

"What?" he asked.

"I was wondering if you could maybe do a favor for me, since I did a favor for you by calling you about your dog?"

James was starting to like the girl. "Okay, payment in kind—fair enough. What do you have in mind, kid?"

"I'm trying to find my mom. She's missing."

He shrugged. "Sorry to hear that. You should go to the cops, then."

Alison rubbed her shoulder. "I did."

"And?"

"They asked a few questions and said they'd get back to us."

James frowned. "Us? As in…"

"My dad and me." She scowled, making it obvious what she thought of her dad.

James decided to ask anyway. Him and his damned stupid curiosity, and desire to know who the good people were in life. "And what about your dad? What's he doing about this?"

An uncomfortable look spread over her face. "My dad's doing his own thing right now."

And which people were just a big bag of dick tips.

Getting involved in non-bounties was always a pain in the ass, and for all James knew, the girl's mom was some junkie whore who had run off to avoid paying her dealer or pimp. But in a world going to shit more and more each year, maybe it'd help to reward a kid who'd gone to the trouble of calling him about his missing dog.

That didn't mean he had to make it easy for the girl.

James stared at her for a moment before cracking a smile. "Finding my dog isn't worth me tracking down your missing mom, kid. I'm a bounty hunter, and I tackle all types of bounties. I could go find myself some rogue-ass Elf assassin in the time it'd take me to track down your mom, and I'd make a shit-ton more money."

Alison waved her hands in front of her. "No, no, no. I don't need you to track my mom down. I just need you to take me to this meeting with these two guys. The Ishidas. They are supposed to know everybody in this area."

The Ishidas? The name didn't ring a bell, and James didn't forget a name.

One perk of a photographic memory.

Alison offered him a bright smile. "All I really need is a quick ride. It saves me having to take a bunch of buses."

This time he raised an eyebrow. "Are you serious, kid? You're going to get in a truck with some random guy you just met?"

"I can tell you're a good guy."

"How?" he gruffed. Not too many could look at him and not think him ugly—and that was the nicest suggestion.

Alison shrugged noncommittally. "I have my ways."

James waved his hand at his face. "None of this scares you? I had a guy tell me once he thought I was half ogre."

He wasn't. At least he was pretty sure he wasn't. He assumed someone would have been able to figure that out from a blood test.

"Why? Should it?" Alison narrowed her eyes as if trying to look closer before shrugging. "And I'm pretty sure you're not a half-ogre, if that's even a thing."

James blinked, stepping back. Most people took one look at the mottled patterns and ridges on his face and freaked out. Of course they did.

He was fucking ugly; had a face only a dog could love—and James was pretty sure Leeroy was half-blind, to boot.

Shit, the girl hadn't even blinked at his voice, which someone once told him sounded like an old jet engine and a steamroller having rough sex.

This normal-ass teen girl didn't even blink. She was either brave, or desperate. He wanted to reward the former, and keep her from making a mistake if she was the latter.

James nodded toward his truck. "Get in on the passenger side."

She eyed the truck. "Probably gonna need help, or a ladder."

"Whatever. Just step forward and I'll pull you up."

"An alley?" James said, shaking his head. "You've got to be fucking kidding me? Are you *trying* to get killed?"

Alison rolled her eyes. "Look, Mr. Brownstone, sometimes you have to dig through garbage when you've lost something important."

"I'm not going to let you meet two guys you heard about on the internet by yourself," James told her.

"If you show up, they might decide to run." Alison bit her lip. "Okay, here…just wait around the corner or something. I'll talk to them, and you will see. Everything will be okay."

James grunted. This whole thing reeked more by the second. He liked the girl's spunk, but she was the absolute definition of naïve. "Whatever. Be careful, kid."

Leeroy whimpered from the back seat.

He reached around and scratched Leeroy behind the ears. "It'll be okay, boy. This will be over soon."

Alison opened the door and hopped out of the truck, landing with a little high-pitched grunt. James chuckled and got out on his side.

He waited, watching her look up and down the street before darting across it toward the alley. Information brokers who hung out in alleys didn't exactly strike him as reputable. The chance that the girl's mother had run away to avoid her dealer had just gone up.

He grunted and looked at the sky. *Why am I here? This shit isn't even my problem.*

Alison entered the alley and James jogged down the street a double handful of steps before crossing. He didn't want anyone in the alley to spot him. Another quick check for drones spotted a few bright security models hovering in the distance near a store, but the walls on either side of the alley stood tall enough to block line of sight.

The Ishidas had selected their location well...which worried him.

James hurried back to the mouth of the alley, flattening himself against a nearby wall and listening.

He could hear her voice. "I have money," she offered. "I can pay if you can help me find my mom."

"So you're Alison Anderson?" a voice asked. Definitely a thick accent; James was no linguist, but it sounded Japanese to him.

"Yeah, and I need your help to find my mom, Nicole Anderson. I was told you were the men to talk to about that."

A mocking laugh echoed in the alley.

"Stupid little girl. You'll come with us now. I'm sure we can find a way for you to make money for our organization—much more than you could pay us."

James' stomach tightened. These guys had earned a future ass-kicking right here, right now.

"No, I don't think so," Alison said. "I came here to get information on my mom, not get kidnapped by you assholes."

The sound of a loud smack echoed in the alley, and Alison cried out.

"You will learn to hold your tongue, girl, or I'll cut it out," one of the men growled.

James rounded the corner.

He'd had enough of this shit.

Two heavily-tattooed Japanese men in dark suits stood over Alison in the middle of the alley. A scabbard sheathed a Japanese short sword, a *wakizashi*, on the belt of each. She knelt on the ground, holding her cheek.

James let out a long sigh. If the men were being this blatant, that meant they had major connections—probably big enough that they didn't worry about cops. That pointed in only one direction: organized crime.

Japanese organized crime in this part of the city was controlled entirely by one gang: the *Harriken*.

The *Harriken*, for when your local Yakuza were too gutless to play.

One of the men looked at James and frowned. "Leave, or you'll end up covered in your own blood."

James recognized him as the first speaker and decided his new name was "Cockbite One." He didn't give a shit which Ishida he was.

"If I wanted to stay clean," James said, his guttural and deep voice resonating in the alley, "I wouldn't have come here to make sure this little girl got home in one piece." He pointed at Cockbite One. "And you're already smacking her around?" He scratched an eyelid. "Let's just say I'm a guy who likes a semi-fair fight. I say 'semi-fair,' because you assholes don't have a chance against me. I'm trying to warn you."

Cockbite Two laughed and indicated Cockbite One. "Do you know who we are, meatbag?"

"Two guys who love to have their asses kicked? Perhaps closet masochists who get their jollies slapping little girls because they can't handle a twenty-year-old without whimpering?"

Cockbite One clucked his tongue. "We are *Harriken*." He leaned back and grinned.

James just stood there for a moment, then shrugged. Cockbite One scowled, pissed that the mere mention of his organization didn't send this guy running.

"We're taking this girl," Cockbite One told him. "I won't warn you again." He stepped back and crossed his arms.

Alison scrambled away from between the guys and ran behind James.

"You idiots aren't kidnapping me," she yelled. "You can kiss my butt."

James chuckled. "You heard the kid."

Every cell in James' body burned for him to humble the assholes, but he knew that antagonizing the *Harriken* wasn't smart, even by his standards. He pulled out his phone.

"Why shouldn't I just call the cops?" James asked, waving his phone.

Cockbite One grinned and held up his arm. "No police will save you here."

James couldn't identify the band on his arm, but assumed it was some sort of jammer. He rolled his eyes.

More lazy tech-obsessed criminals.

He had expected more from the Harriken. They were supposed to be an old-school Japanese clan with some weird-ass warrior honor.

He slid the phone back in his pocket. "Whatever. More fun for me."

Cockbite One's face darkened. "Enough of this foolishness. This is Harriken territory, and you have been disrespectful. You *will* be made into an example, for those who dare oppose our power. If you beg," he smirked, "we'll kill you quickly."

James sucked in a breath through his teeth. "Did anyone in your little group ever tell you about the Granite Ghost?"

He removed his leather jacket and dropped it to the ground, not caring that it revealed his holster and sheaths. He wouldn't even bother to use the weapons for this pathetic level of foe. He was mostly concerned they might damage his jacket.

He really loved that jacket.

Cockbite One snorted. "A child's story." He whipped out his sword. "You're going to die today, and become a *real* ghost."

Alison laughed. "Oh, you guys don't even see it, do you? He's so gonna kick your asses. Too much testosteronie, boys. It's bad for decision-making."

"It's 'testosterone,'" James looked at her, "and who is teaching you these words?"

Cockbite One snarled. "After I kill this man in front of you, little girl, you'll be coming with me." He pointed at Allison. "And I will tape that smart mouth of yours shut."

James sighed. "Don't worry, I've got this." He put his hand on her shoulder and pushed her toward a wooden box by the wall. "Just step back."

Cockbite Two readied his blade.

Maybe there was still a way to salvage the situation that didn't involve copious amounts of ultra-violence. James hoped so, at least.

Well, not exactly.

It wasn't that he cared about hurting these assholes—he didn't mind taking down people who deserved it—but killing people, even scum, complicated his life...and that violated KISS.

"Okay, guys," James began, cracking his knuckles. "Here's my rules. You stay with swords and knives and I'll smack you around, but you get to leave alive, if broken. You go any higher than that, and you might not be breathing at the end. Don't say I didn't warn you."

"You die now!" Cockbite One yelled. He charged right toward James, his sword slicing downward.

James brought up his arm. The ring of metal meeting metal echoed through the alley.

Cockbite One leapt back, and Cockbite Two moved forward.

"Armor?" Cockbite One said with a sneer. "That's why you're so disrespectful?" He spat. "We'll just take your head off, then."

James heaved another sigh, looking at the clean slice in his gray shirt. He'd just gotten the thing, and the asshole had already carved it up.

Both Harriken charged him this time. For a few seconds they all traded blows, blocks, and parries. James smirked as their swords struck him again and again, not doing much more than making the alley sound like some drunken blacksmith's shop.

James' shirt was in tatters at this point, but there wasn't a single drop of blood in sight.

One of the men tossed his sword into his other hand and reached inside his jacket to pull out a Glock. It took James a second to realize it was Cockbite Two.

James groaned; some idiots never learned. He concentrated for a second.

The pistol sailed out of the man's hand and into James'. A little telekinesis could go a long way toward stopping a bloodbath, but today the situation was going in the opposite direction.

"I told you that you could walk out of here," James rumbled, "if you didn't go there." He slowly bent the gun in half and tossed it to the ground.

The man's eyes widened. "What are you, an *oni?*"

James shrugged. "Is that some kind of half-ogre?"

Cockbite One swung his sword, hoping to take advantage of his opponent's distraction, and James caught the blade with his bare hand. Not even a scratch.

"Alison is here," James said, "so I'm concerned about shedding too much of your blood. You know, 'kids are impressionable' and all that shit."

"Don't worry about me," she called from behind James. "You know how many violent movies and VR sims the average kid sees? Last time I checked, it was something like twenty thousand simulated murders and hundreds of thousands of acts of violence by the age of eighteen. Maybe it'll be educational to see the difference between real and fake." She smirked. "Or maybe I'm just willing to take the chance that I won't be horribly traumatized by the deaths of you two buttholes right in front of me."

"Shut your mouth, *baka shi youjo!*" Cockbite One screamed, in fury both because James had caught his weapon and the girl wasn't afraid.

James had no idea what *"baka shi youjo"* meant, but he doubted it was a compliment. He casually backhanded Cockbite One, and the Japanese mobster sailed through the air to slam into a wall twelve feet away. The crunch of bone echoed through the alley.

"And I didn't even hit him as hard as I wanted to," James

commented. He glared at the other man. "Do you wanna keep going? I mean, shit, man, I think I've proven you can't do crap to me."

"Fucking *oni*," Cockbite Two snarled, trembling with rage. He pointed his sword toward James as he backed up. "You have signed your death warrant. The Harriken will hunt you down, kill your family, and slice your dick off and feed it to you."

"Get the fuck out of here before I punt you through a wall," James replied. "Besides, if I kill your ass here, who is going to tell the Harriken to go cut my dick off and feed it to me? You have to think these things through, motherfucker."

The Harriken moved toward the wall and grabbed his buddy, then dragged him out of the alley.

James exhaled and shook his head. He'd stepped in it for sure, but sometimes the best way to KISS was to go all-in.

No nuances meant no misunderstandings.

James grabbed his jacket and slipped it back on. He glanced at Alison, who was looking around, eyes slightly unfocused.

"You've got a mouth on you, kid," James said. "Not that those assholes didn't have it coming." He nodded toward the entrance to the alley. "Let's get out of here, in case they bring back some friends who might actually cause me to break a sweat."

2

They drove in silence several minutes. James wasn't angry with Alison, but he was pissed at the Ishidas for destroying his new shirt. Maybe he could bill the Harriken somehow.

He chuckled at the thought.

"What's your address?" he asked. "I should get you home."

Alison rattled it off. "Thanks for saving me."

He turned right on La Cienega. "Be smarter next time, kid."

She looked toward him. "I brought you, didn't I?"

As he shrugged, the remnants of his shirt knotted up inside his jacket. "Good point."

James revved his engine to take a corner aggressively. Nothing calmed him like that sound.

"And what's with all the stats?" he said. "Is that the kind of shit they teach in school nowadays?" He didn't remember any of the nuns at his school throwing those kinds of numbers at him.

Maybe if they had, I wouldn't have ended up such a violent man.

"I don't have a teacher, Mr. Brownstone," Alison replied.

He spared a glance her way. "Why don't you have a teacher?"

"I don't go to school."

His eyes narrowed. "You don't go to school?"

"Nope."

James shrugged. "Huh. You don't seem like an idiot, though."

"I'm kind of home-schooled. My mom helped, but I do a lot of it myself."

As he turned another corner, he checked his mirrors for suspicious vehicles, drones, or shimmering spots of air. It was hard to guess anymore what kind of tools an individual criminal group might utilize, mystical or otherwise.

Satisfied that he wasn't about to be tac-nuked by a zombie dragon, James returned his attention to Alison. "Why don't you go to school?"

"Mom didn't really want me to, and they don't have good resources for people with issues like mine."

He snorted. "What, smart-ass syndrome?"

Alison let out a quiet sigh. "Uh, no. Haven't you figured it out, Mr. Brownstone?" She paused for a moment. "I'm blind."

James glanced at her. Now that she mentioned it, the slightly unfocused look in her eyes did remind him of a blind person's, and when he'd helped her into the truck earlier she'd patted around as if she were making sure the truck was there. But a lot of things still didn't make sense.

"You can't be blind," James argued. "I've seen you walk and respond to shit."

"I do when it has energy, Mr. Brownstone. I see the energy, and understand what it is. I didn't find your dog because he ran up to me, I found your dog because he was scared and I saw his energy flare. It's kind of like seeing his fear."

"Shit, really?" James shook his head. In his line of work he ran into the unusual all the time, so he had no reason to doubt the girl. Hell, he himself was pretty damned unusual for a human.

"Yeah, really." Alison smiled and shrugged. "I can read braille as well. I have a cool haptic reader Mom got me."

"Haptic?" James asked.

"It means 'touch feedback.' The surface changes, so I can load an ebook and read it in braille. Or I can listen, but I read faster than narrators speak."

James chuckled a little at the teenage girl knowing fancier words than he did. This little side trip had already become way more involved than he'd planned, though. He needed to get the girl back to her father.

He frowned. "Before we go anywhere else, we need to talk about your dad. I figure he knew you were looking into this, and I'm a pretty shitty adult to let you meet shady fucks in an alley, but here goes nothing: does your father have a clue where you are?"

"He has a clue, in the sense that he knows I'm looking for Mom," Alison admitted. "Not that he cares, because he hasn't looked for Mom in the three weeks since she mysteriously disappeared and the cops left."

"Wait, is that what you meant by 'he's doing his thing?'"

Alison's slender hands curled into fists. "I don't even know where he is. He took off last week. Left some money for food and told me he had to take care of some business stuff." She snorted. "Business stuff? That loser can barely count."

"Is he even your dad?"

"Only because he's married to Mom. Otherwise, he's a sperm donor," she replied caustically.

James grunted. He didn't have much to say about that. Growing up in an orphanage meant he didn't know crap about fathers who weren't the Catholic priest kind.

Alison was obviously a capable young woman, but the timing with the dad screamed "suspicious."

"Do you think your dad did something to your Mom?"

Alison turned to face him. It was still hard for him to wrap his mind around the fact that she was technically blind. "Oh, I *know* he did something. Let me guess, you want to know how I know?"

James pulled to a stop at a red light, nodding. It was like Alison could read his mind.

"It's the energy, Mr. Brownstone. People give off tons of it. When Mom disappeared, his energy turned black."

"Maybe he was just worried," James replied.

"Wrong color for that," Alison told him, looking down. She lifted her head. "It's also how I know you're a good guy."

He snorted. "It's because you can't see my ugly-ass face."

"You're right, I can't. I see the true you. If there's any blessing that comes from my special sight, it's that I see the purity of everyone's heart."

"Then my heart must be stone-cold black."

Alison furiously shook her head. "No, Mr. Brownstone, it is the most beautiful color I've ever seen."

What the fuck? The kid really was blind.

———————

What does that mean anyway? How the hell do I have a beautiful heart?

Alison's revelation shut James right up until he arrived in front of her house, a modest white one-story with peeling paint. Weeds were waging war with the grass in the lawn, and James figured they were going to overcome the last vestiges by next month.

"Are you gonna be all right here by yourself?" he asked.

"I've been all right for a week. Why wouldn't I continue to be?"

James frowned, but didn't say anything. He'd already gotten far more involved than he should have—and a girl like her might end up in trouble if they punted her into the social services system, especially since her abilities were unusual. More than a few corrupt assholes inside and outside the government might want to sell a girl who could see into people's hearts.

James pulled out his wallet and handed her a business card. Raised sigils lined the border of the card.

"It's a one-use card," he explained. "It'll get to me no matter what, and I'll know exactly where you are when you use it. But you can only use it once, so use it wisely. Otherwise, just call me on the number you used to tell me about

Leeroy. I might answer the phone, or I might not." He scratched the side of his head. "I… Well, shit! I guess you might need help using it. I didn't think to make a braille version."

Alison smirked and slipped the card into her pocket. "I'll figure something out. Thanks again for everything, Mr. Brownstone." She reached into the back to pat the sleeping Leeroy. While his master had been busy fighting Japanese mobsters, the loyal dog had fallen asleep.

Hardly the stuff that epic *Hachi*-style canine legends were made of.

The girl opened the door and carefully hopped down from the truck. James watched as she made her way toward her door, amazed that she could navigate so well with her odd combination of blindness and energy-sensing. Still, if what she had said wasn't bullshit, she possessed truer sight than most people.

Just who was that girl?

The whole revelation made him wonder. He didn't even understand where *his* abilities came from, and he was human. Oriceran had changed everything. The old world order was dead.

Just, no one wanted to admit it yet.

Taking a deep breath, James threw his F-350 into gear to head back to his own place. He hoped the girl would be okay, but he'd already done more than enough to help her.

He pulled away from the curb and rolled down the road.

He revved his engine.

There was one thing he could always count on, and that was the wonderful feeling of power he got when he revved his old Ford. Los Angeles was infested with electric cars, and he wondered how long it would take before people started puttering around on magic carpets woven with Oriceran magic or using wings.

Fifteen minutes brought him to his house, an older wood-frame place. Plenty of space for him, and a nice upstairs loft he used for storage.

James picked up the sleeping Leeroy and headed toward his front door. He wondered how his dog had gotten out, and so far away from his property.

"You better not secretly be a shifter, Leeroy," he muttered. "And if you are, you better damn well explain why you've shit or pissed inside so many times instead of using the bathroom."

He set the snoozing dog down. Leeroy woke up and stretched for a moment before letting out a happy bark.

James fished a key out of his pocket and unlocked his door. Most people on his block had gone to smart locks—more tech to hack and fail. Extender drones could even do it remotely.

At least with a physical lock, you had to kick it open. Or blow it open. Both made noise, though—and noise would alert him that someone was there to kill him.

He opened the door, and Leeroy ran in.

"Stick around this time, dog," James called after him.

He took off his boots. A closet stood right next to the front door, and shoes and boots sat in a neat line on a multi-tiered shoe rack inside. He set his boots in an obvious hole in the line.

James glanced around as he walked farther into the

house. Every pile of papers was where it should be. He ran his hand along the wall…no dust.

He chuckled to himself. A stupidly clean house was what happened when you didn't have any other real hobbies. Plus, it gave him something to do when he was watching cooking shows on television, or listening to barbeque podcasts.

James stepped into his living room and pulled a painting of Saint Jerome to the side. There was a sealed weapons locker with a palm sensor in an alcove behind the painting. Violating KISS annoyed him, but some things he wouldn't risk. He placed his hand on the sensor, and the locker clicked open.

He put his knife and gun inside, then slipped off his necklace, eyeing it for a moment. He put it in the locker and closed it. He didn't want to wear that thing unless he had to.

James headed to a black leather recliner in his living room and dropped into it, then pulled out his phone and brought up the LAPD Bounty Hunter Outreach Department app.

Spending all day helping smart-mouthed little girls and enraging Japanese mobsters might be fun, but it didn't the pay the bills.

He tapped away, scanning through the available bounties. Mostly low-level cases, Level Ones and Twos, mostly humans. Barely worth leaving home for. A few rogue-troll wrangles—those might be worthwhile. He felt bad, though, because the trolls got in trouble too, and it was mostly the assholes who bonded with them who were responsible for them turning dangerous.

A nice, even-tempered person bonded to a troll might end up with nothing more than an annoying pet. On the other hand, a psychopathic criminal gangbanger might end up with a walking killer yeti to throw at his enemies, if a troll were willing to bond with such a person. Trolls were damned smart; much smarter than they got credit for. Only in very rare cases would they connect with shitty people.

But when they did...that was where the "bad troll" stories came from.

James tossed his phone on a small table next to his chair and picked up his remote. He didn't give a shit how old-school using a remote instead of voice-control made him. The damn machines didn't understand his deep voice, for whatever reason.

He glanced at his watch. Yeah, about time for his favorite show, *Barbecue Wars: New Generation.* A few clicks brought it up.

"I don't know, Jill," said one of the judges. It was Henry, an elderly Asian man with white hair. "I'm a barbecue purist, and I don't know or trust a sauce made using ingredients not native to this world. I mean, we're not talking South Carolina versus North Carolina, we're talking Earth versus Oriceran."

Jill, the show's token perky blonde floor reporter, shook her head. "We don't see a lot of non-human competitors on *Barbecue Wars: New Generation,* so I'm excited to see what *magic* this Elf pit-master can bring to the competition." She winked.

James grimaced. "KISS!" he shouted. "Magic isn't fucking simple!"

Sure, it could be useful, but it was never *simple*.

Leeroy barked in response.

He scrubbed a hand across his face. If he'd been born thirty years earlier, he wouldn't have to deal with this barbecue sacrilege.

3

James slammed the truck's door closed and stepped over the cobblestone path that led to a simple stone church nestled among several huge ash trees.

He smiled to himself as he gazed at the stone, which was worn by the wind and the rain. For two centuries, the church had stood in a land that had passed through the hands of different countries. Nations came and went, but the Catholic Church was eternal, and this specific church was well on its way to that status as well.

To the bounty hunter, there was nothing simpler than a Catholic church. You knew exactly what to expect when you entered one, and what kind of people might be inside. This contrasted with the Church itself, one of the most complicated social organizations in history.

James opened the door and made his way through the mostly empty nave. A few older Mexican women sat in the back pews, and they glanced up at him briefly before returning to their silent prayers as he continued toward the confessional. On arrival, he carefully opened his side and stepped in before sliding the door closed.

"Bless me, Father, for I have sinned," James began. "It has been one week since my last confession."

"Go on, child," said a familiar voice. Even with the screen up, James recognized the voice of the elderly Father McCartney. His New Jersey accent was unmistakable, no matter how formally he was speaking.

"I've experienced great wrath," James said, "besides enjoying smacking around some of the bounties. Yesterday, I helped a girl who found my dog."

"Nothing wrong with helping a girl. That doesn't sound very wrathful."

"This girl was looking for her mom, and she set up a meeting with some shady sh—" James gritted his teeth. He wouldn't profane this place. "Some shady men. It turns out they were Harriken."

He didn't need to explain. Father McCartney was many things, but he wasn't naïve about the evil that stalked the world—human or otherwise.

"They tried to take the girl," James continued. "They did not...respond to my attempts at peaceful negotiation."

"Of course they didn't." The priest sighed. "I see, child. And did you take the men's lives?"

"No, I didn't, even though they threatened the girl and tried to pull a gun on me, and it would have been justified. Instead I really hurt them, and I'll admit I enjoyed it."

James resisted smirking, even though he was proud of what he'd done.

"The Harriken are dangerous, child. It might not be wise to stoke their wrath."

"Scum infest the city. Scum infest the world." James shrugged. "Someone has to push back."

"There's some truth to that, but as the Gospel of Matthew teaches us, those who will take up the sword will die by the sword."

James coughed. "Just want to remind you that I didn't kill anybody—although they really, *really* had it coming."

"The righteous warrior will smite the wicked and the enemies of the Lord," the priest intoned, "but he must always be wary of letting wrath and vainglory into his heart, for it will turn him into the monsters he faces."

James didn't know about that, but he wasn't going to argue with a priest about what God wanted.

"You are blessed by the Lord, child. He has touched you in this time of tribulation, and given you a special purpose. The veils between the worlds have worn thin, and evil walks our planet with strange powers. Use your talents wisely, as you have done in defense of those who are weak. Blessed are the meek, for they shall inherit the Earth."

"I guess I'm not going be part of that crew," James muttered.

"And what of the girl?" the priest asked.

"I took her home. I think she's living by herself, but she isn't starving or anything. Her mother is gone, and her father might be involved in the disappearance. The cops have already been worthless. Big fu—uh, big surprise."

"I see. Then it might be best for you to keep an eye on her."

James snorted. "I don't have a lot of time to babysit." He sighed. "Look, I gave her a one-use card, and she's got my number. If she gets in trouble, she'll call me. Good enough?"

"For now." Father McCartney chuckled quietly. "If you're paying attention to her, not much more I can ask."

"Yeah." James slid open the booth. He needed to escape before the priest put him in charge of a busload of orphans.

Cowardly? Sure.

But even he couldn't win against God.

At the Leanan Sídhe, his favorite Irish pub, James sat across a table from a white-haired man with a couple of decades on him, the Professor—or at least that was what James called him.

Officially he was Doctor F.J. Smite-Williams, Professor of Historical Extra-Dimensional Engineering, which was a fancy way of saying he studied magical artifacts.

If you got a few drinks in him he liked to go by Father O'Banion, which amused James on some days and annoyed him on others.

They hadn't met in a while, but James wanted to keep up his contacts—especially those outside the Church or the police.

"I might be able to line up something for you soon, lad," the older man told him. He leaned back, resting his hands on his slightly pudgy middle. He'd already downed more than a few beers before James' arrival, leaving his cheeks even ruddier than usual. "I'm just running down a few more contacts."

James swallowed a sip of his Irish Stout. "This isn't another bullshit run, is it?"

The Professor laughed and shook his head. "Sorry about that, lad, but you never know. It could have turned out to be the Holy Grail." He sipped some of his own beer, a Harp Lager. "And we can't be having just anyone get their hands on something like that, human or otherwise. Too many artifacts are spilling out onto the streets as it is." A huge grin appeared on his face. "These times of chaos are interesting, but also damned dangerous."

James shrugged and drank more of his beer. "Not disagreeing. Just make sure it's worth my time. Been doing too much free shit lately."

"Like picking fights with the Harriken?" The Professor let out a merry chuckle.

"It seems like everyone has heard about that."

"You sure know how to make friends."

James smirked. "Guess it's my wonderful personality. I didn't figure the Harriken would go blabbing so much about their guys getting their asses kicked."

"They didn't, but people are always watching these days, one way or another."

James thought that over. From what he could remember, no surveillance drones had had line of sight on the alley, but that didn't mean some magical spy bee hadn't been flying cloaked overhead.

The Professor leaned forward, a bright smile still on his face. "Just remember, lad, that organizations like that can call on allies. It's not some tiny fool playing at being a big man because his uncle gave him a magic ring."

James grunted. "What, you worried about me?"

"I'm more worried about local property values." The Professor's eyes glinted in humor.

"Don't worry about me. Just let me know about your lead."

"Will do, lad."

A dog barked in the corner, and a customer handed the dog an open bottle. The Amazing Malty was one of the bar's attractions. Malty grabbed the bottle with his paws, upended it and started chugging.

"Chug, chug, chug," everyone in the bar started chanted in unison. The Professor shouted louder than anyone.

James didn't join the chant. He waited until Malty was done with his beer and chuckled.

"That dog is more hardcore than I am." He turned back to face the Professor.

Smite-Williams shook his head. "That's sad, lad. You shouldn't be outdone by a dog."

James shrugged. "He gives more of a shit. No big deal." He finished his beer. "I should get going. I need to make sure my dog's not stealing *my* beer."

"I'm sure he has much better taste than that."

James threw the door open of his house and called, "Leeroy, buddy! Let's go for a walk!"

No response. No eager bark. No *thump, thump, thump* of the dog charging through the house.

"Leeroy?" James called again. He frowned. "You've got to be fucking kidding me."

He searched the house and confirmed his fear. Leeroy was nowhere to be found.

No obvious holes in the wall or ceiling presented themselves as possible escape routes. Fifteen minutes of searching brought the bounty hunter back to his living room, which conspicuously lacked one foolish black lab.

James ran his hands over his bald head. When it came to normal bounties he was good at thinking like a criminal, but he had no idea how to think like a damned dog.

Leeroy could be anywhere. He'd managed to make it fifteen minutes away by car last time, where he somehow got his useless ass stuck in a drainpipe.

Damn it, Leeroy. How did you get out again? Why can't you just be satisfied, dog?

Well, the best strategy when you've lost something is to start looking where you last saw it. James had already tried the house, so it was time to move on to the second-to-last place.

He pulled out his phone and dialed Alison.

"Mr. Brownstone?" she answered.

"Hey, Alison. You didn't happen to find my dog in a drainpipe again, did you?"

"Leeroy is missing?"

"Yeah."

Alison sighed. "Sorry. I've barely left home since yesterday. I haven't seen him."

"No problem. It was a long shot, anyway."

"I'm sorry, Mr. Brownstone. I'm really sorry."

"Too bad you can't track with that magic vision of yours," James said. "And don't worry about it. This isn't the first time I've had trouble with Leeroy escaping. I'll find him." He chuckled. "Last time I ended up having to fight Harriken, though."

She laughed quietly on the other end. "I think they regretted it more than you did."

"Sometimes it's good to remind monsters that there are always bigger monsters out there." He paused in a moment of consideration. "Though now that I've said that shit, some dragon's probably gonna eat me."

The girl's smile faded and she shook her head, although he obviously couldn't see her. "You're not a monster, Mr. Brownstone."

"Sure I am, kid. I'm the monster you point at other monsters, kind of like how sometimes Godzilla's good and sometimes he's bad."

"You forget, I can see your heart," she reminded him.

"Then you need to get your magic eyes checked, kid. I've done a lot of brutal things in my life."

"And have you ever hurt anyone who didn't have it coming?"

He pursed his lips. "That's all a matter of perspective, kid."

James furrowed his brow. He didn't have time to debate with a teenager as to where he fell on the Sonofabitch scale. His dog was missing—one of the few creatures he'd ever run into who loved him unconditionally. Plenty of people respected his strength, but that was just another way of being afraid of a monster.

Delusions were for the weak. Being human didn't make him any less of a monster than some of those wacked-out magical assholes from Oriceran.

"If you see him, give me a call," James requested. "I'm going to go ask around the neighborhood."

"Okay." She hung up, and he slipped his phone back into his pocket.

A trip to James' closet netted him a sheath and a shoulder holster. He returned to his living room to move the painting of Saint Jerome aside to access his weapons locker, from which he retrieved a .45 and a K-Bar. That should be enough for neighborhood interviews.

He went toward the door. "Now to find my dog."

Two hours later, James pulled his F-350 up to his third street corner. Several gangbangers wearing matching bandanas loitered in the area, most leaning against a wall trying their best to look intimidating. It might have worked on someone who couldn't punch a man into a wall several yards away.

They were a far less hospitable crowd than the old ladies at the first street corner or the school kids at the second street corner.

Not that James worried. These guys were teddy bears compared to the Harriken—almost a joke in today's dangerous world. They were a vestige of another time that wanted to pretend it still had relevance.

James rolled down his window.

The gangbangers pushed off the wall, surrounding the truck in a semi-circle, and squaring their shoulders.

Now, if they dared hurt his truck, James would have to

have a one-way conversation with them that might involve typing a few exclamation points using his knuckles.

"Hey, guys," James rumbled. "Trey, that you back there?"

One of the older gangbangers sauntered forward, a cigarette dangling from his mouth. "Fucking Mr. Brownstone." The man gave him a comically exaggerated bow. "Haven't seen you around for a while. I mean, I've seen your sweet-ass ride, but you don't talk with the peasants enough, man."

"Sorry." James shrugged. "Been busy kicking people's asses."

"Yeah, so I hear." He eyed the man in the truck. "I've been hearing shit about you. Crazy shit."

"I'm a bounty hunter who goes after high-value bounties. Crazy's in the job description."

Trey grinned. "This is more like local shit."

James laughed. "Like what?"

"They say you pissed off the Harriken, man...big time. That they be planning to come for you."

I'd like to see that. How many of those assholes do I need to smash into a wall for them to get the point?

James shrugged. "It's more like they pissed *me* off and then happened to get in the way of my fist, and then a wall got in their way. Real sad for them, boring for me. Plus, they owe me a new shirt."

Trey shook his head and looked over his shoulder for a second. "Just saying, watch your back, man. Harriken probably do some dragon-magic kung fu shit."

"Yeah, yeah. Whatever."

The gangbanger stared at him. "You ain't here to score, are you? You never are." He shook a finger. "When you don't contribute to the local economy, man, you're undermining the community and all that shit."

"I don't need drugs, and how the hell do you understand the nuances of commercialism, drugs, and the local economy? Besides, ultra-violence is my anti-drug." James shrugged.

Trey groaned. "But we got better shit nowadays. Some of the stuff they are supplying now... Man, the Oriceran shit's like a brave new world, motherfucker. Makes LSD look like somethin' you should give a baby in a bottle."

He looked at Trey, bored. "I don't give a crap about that."

"Then why you here, Mr. Brownstone?"

"I just wanted to know if you've seen my dog." He pulled out a picture of the black lab from his wallet.

Trey motioned for the rest of the gang members to get closer so they could see the picture.

"Your dog?" Trey brow furrowed. "Name's like Leelo or some shit, right?"

James grunted. "'Leeroy,' and nothing to do with *The Fifth Element*. Damn, who's watching classics? He's got tags. If you find him, you know where I live. An award can be arranged."

The gangbanger shook his head, then looked at his friends. "Any of you seen Mr. Brownstone's dog?"

Everyone shrugged or shook their heads.

"Man," Trey waved at the guys, "all you bitches are useless." He pointed to the picture. "If you see his dog, you tell me right away. If you see anyone fucking with his dog, you beat their asses."

"Thanks, Trey," James told him sincerely.

Trey saluted James. "Keep doing what you do, man. Make the world a better place and all that shit."

James rolled up the window and pulled away from the curb. Low-level gang crap didn't pique his interest. If an individual gang member got out of hand maybe he'd give a crap, but for the most part, he tried not to shit where he lived.

He was no closer to finding his dog, though. It was time for stop four.

Lachlan, one of Trey's newest recruits, pushed off the wall and headed toward his leader.

"Did you see that sweet-ass shit he was driving?" Lachlan said.

Trey shrugged. "It's a truck. It's sweet, sure, but it's still just an old truck."

"No, it's a classic Ford F-350. That shit is old-school, and like you said, it was sweet. I mean, every time I seen one, they all fucked up and dented and shit." Lachlan patted the Glock resting in the waistband of the back of his pants. "Why didn't we carjack that lame-ass motherfucker and take his sweet-ass truck? Bitch comes over here crying over his dog? Since when are we the damn pound?"

Every other gangbanger stopped chatting and stared at Lachlan like he'd pissed on their mothers. Several glared openly. One even had his hand on the handle of his gun.

Lachlan blinked. "What? Who is that motherfucker? He connected, or some shit? 'Mr. Brownstone?' Sounds like some bitch algebra teacher."

Trey slapped Lachlan upside the head. "That's the motherfucking Granite Ghost, home-bitch! James Brownstone. You do *not* want to be fucking with James Brownstone unless you've got a death wish."

Lachlan swallowed, doing his best not to tremble in front of his gang brothers. "Wait, that shit ain't real. That's just a story. They ain't no such thing as the Granite Ghost."

Trey looked up toward his great-grandma, who was staring down at him from heaven, to ask her for just a little fucking patience. He looked back at Lachlan. "He's the real-fucking-deal, dumbass. He takes down major bounties, man. Human, non-human, magical, or whatever. The guy's a living tank. I wouldn't be surprised if the government drops him into foreign countries to clear out terrorists and shit." Trey shook his head. "They say he's human, but no one really knows, man."

"My cousin Marco," yelled another gang member, "he told me how Brownstone's some sort of magic gargoyle or some shit the Pope brought to life to fight demons. It's the Apocalypse, motherfucker, and the Vatican ain't playing."

Another man scoffed. "I don't know about that, but a smart guy I know from Arleta told me that they drained a bunch of blood out of Light Elves and like injected it into him as part of some Army experiment. Like Captain-Fucking-America but with magic, right?"

"Nah, man," another gangbanger spoke up. "That ain't it. He was like this dude, just minding his own business, and some guy robbed and shot him. They said he was so pissed that when he got to hell, Satan let him come back and wreak vengeance. They say if he reaps like 666 sinners' souls he gets to go to heaven, and that's why he started bounty hunting."

Lachlan scoffed. "That's bullshit. None of that's true."

Trey tapped his ears. "We got motherfucking Elves casting spells and shit now. My mom knows a motherfucking Witch, and you saying James ain't a gargoyle or a ghost? Who gives a fuck? You know what's true? He kicks ass." He gestured in the direction James had driven. "Two Harriken got their ass beat by him. He smashed one dude into the wall."

"If he's so tough, why can't he find his dog?"

"He's tough, motherfucker." Trey shook his head, tossing another prayer to his great-grandma. "Not a damn psychic."

"So what if he got lucky against some sword freaks? That don't prove shit."

Trey fished his phone out of his pocket. "Mr. Brownstone let me keep this video, as long as I didn't put it up on the net." He tapped around on his phone for few moments, then held it up. "Seeing's believing, motherfucker."

A half-dozen bikers surrounded James in a parking lot. A couple of them rushed at him and two quick punches sent them flying out of frame, a distance of easily ten feet. A flurry of punches and kicks followed, each ending with either a biker knocked clean out of the viewing frame or smashed into the ground with disturbing force. The short clip ended with James punting one of the larger bikers from the parking lot through a window fifteen feet away.

Lachlan winced. "Fuck."

"You still want to jack his ride, bitch?" Trey asked with a sneer.

The other guy shook his head.

Trey slipped his phone back into his pocket. "If Mr. Brownstone is looking for you, just go talk to him. If you run, he will kick your ass extra-hard for making him work. If it ain't a bounty he's after, he doesn't care what you do...unless you do something to his friends. And if you have?" He shook his head. "Just walk into the police department and surrender. At least then there will be bars between you and him, unless you want to be his latest football."

Lachlan swallowed and fell to his knees, shaking. He'd almost pulled a gun when Brownstone was talking to his leader. He'd thought it'd be a great way to prove he wasn't a pussy.

He hadn't realized how close he'd come to death.

"That's right." Trey wore a satisfied grin. "No one *smart* fucks with Mr. Brownstone."

4

The small light-blue house looked like any other ranch-style home on the palm-lined street. It could have easily been one of thousands of houses in the greater metro area.

James could almost admire that. Being unobtrusive was one of the best ways not to get killed.

He snorted.

Not that he'd been all that shy lately.

James pulled his Ford into the driveway, taking several deep breaths. A faint feeling tugged at the edge of his awareness, most likely some sort of security spell. He wasn't doing a raid so he wasn't worried, but that meant the woman inside the house knew he was coming and would be ready for him in a far more annoying way.

Hell, given the occupant, James would have preferred to have just been shot at.

That only fed into the bounty hunter's existing irritation, the main feeling fueling him. James had spent hours looking for Leeroy, with no damn success. Maybe if he'd found his dog, he would have been less pissed at having to drive all the way out to Pasadena.

James sucked in a deep breath. With a potential big job coming up, he didn't have much choice. As much as he didn't trust magic, sometimes it kept things simpler—especially when all you had to do was drink something.

"Damn potions," James muttered, throwing open the door of his truck.

Being unprepared in this world meant signing your death warrant, and he had a lot of ass to kick before he could take the long dirt nap.

James checked his phone again, just in case he'd somehow hallucinated the earlier text from Smite-Williams.

Got the info. Job is a go. Come by the Leanan Sídhe tonight, if you're interested. This is time-sensitive, and you'll be working under someone else. Show up at 9.

James didn't care if he had to take a few orders. The Professor wouldn't set him up with an idiot partner. The guy might be a horrible boozer, but he was whip-smart, knew the right people, and had the best contacts.

A few quick steps brought James to the house's front door. He raised his fist to knock, but hesitated as his stomach knotted.

Is there any way this won't be annoying as shit?

The door swung open to reveal a young olive-skinned woman in a thin white silk robe. A sensual smile covered her face, and her long and wild dark hair hung to her waist.

"Hey there, lover," the woman said. Her words were slurred, and her gray eyes were bloodshot. She twirled a tapered and stoppered translucent glass bottle in her delicate fingers.

"Hey, Zoe," James said. "Long time no see."

She motioned him inside. "You didn't call ahead, you naughty boy." Her breath reeked of alcohol. Then again, it always did.

"You're a hard woman to get hold of." James stepped in. "And when I do, half the time you're drunk off your shit and babbling gibberish. I never know whether there's any point in even leaving a message, you know?"

Zoe giggled and shrugged. "Guilty as charged on all counts, Your Honor." She winked. "But come on, James, don't be like that. The cost of brewing my potions is that I have to make my own little sacrifice to the spirits...of spirits." She shrugged, and smiled at her joke.

"Yeah, nice excuse for getting smashed all the time." James grunted. "If you weren't the best potions maker in Los Angeles I wouldn't put up with your bullshit, you know."

She laughed. "Oh, just listen to you. It's so adorable when you act irritated, and also when you play hard-to-get."

Potted herbs and flowers covered almost every square inch of the living room, with only a few chairs and a faded brown loveseat breaking up the garden. Thick herbal smells clashed in his nostrils. The individual smells might have been tolerable—or even pleasant—but in combination they made James want to gag.

The witch sashayed past the living room to the dining room, which also played host to a variety of plants, including several hanging from overhead hooks. Most looked normal enough, but several glowed. More than a few tendrils and leaves displayed bright geographical lines and other unexpected patterns.

One had a raised ouroboros glowing on a leaf. James didn't even want to know what sort of messed-up magical plant it was.

He also doubted Zoe had all the necessary permits for growing non-Earth plants, though she probably cared about that as much as he cared about registering all his magical equipment.

The witch set her blue bottle down on a simple round wooden table in the center of the room, where several other stoppered glass bottles of different sizes and colors rested next to a mortar and pestle. Dozens of stoppered vials filled with different-colored fluids sat in a rack near the side of the table.

Zoe tilted her head and leaned against the table, letting her bare leg slip out of her robe. James ignored the flesh and concentrated on her face.

He didn't have time for her little games today.

"You know what I'm here for," James told her. "You still owe me for handling that...whatever the fuck that plant monster was."

"You're truly my hero." Zoe snatched a small vial filled with a dull red liquid from the rack. "Healing." She grabbed a translucent yellow liquid. "Energy." She tossed both the vials at the bounty hunter.

James grabbed them out of the air with a frown. After examining them, he slipped them into his jacket packet.

Zoe stumbled, almost crashing into the potion-covered table. She shrugged and smirked. "The Dionysian Way might leave me a little…happy at times, but you can't argue with the results." She ran a hand up her robe, lingering on her ample breasts. "You know, there's other ways to get me to work for you." She licked her lips. "Much more enjoyable ways than fighting."

"I'm not gonna fuck you, Zoe, so stop asking."

She stuck out her bottom lip in a pout. "You're so mean."

James frowned. He didn't get why Zoe insisted on screwing with him so much. There was no way she was truly interested in him.

The bounty hunter held no illusions about the ugly-ass face he'd been cursed with. It was nothing more than a drunken game for the woman—or so he figured.

He wouldn't deny that she was attractive, but she was about as far from his type as he could imagine, and that was saying something considering he didn't even know what "his type" was.

"Besides," James added, "aren't you a little old for me?"

Zoe sniggered. "Oh, you finally found that out?" She shrugged a single shoulder. "Not that I was trying to hide it."

"It's bullshit anyway." James motioned at her. "You're a witch. Aren't you supposed to be ugly?"

Her face scrunched in confusion. "Whyever would that be?"

"You know, shouldn't you have warts and green skin?"

Zoe rolled her eyes. "Don't be so last century, James." She leaned forward, her voice seductive as she said, "I promise you, the carpet matches the drapes. And nothing, and I mean *nothing*, is green."

Okay, that was enough. James was done with her shit.

"Thanks for the potions, Zoe." He pivoted on his heel and headed straight for the front door.

"I'm not the only one with secrets, James," Zoe called to him.

He stopped and looked over his shoulder. "What are you getting at?"

"Don't you remember why you first came to me, James?"

James grit his teeth. "Because you're the best, as fucking irritating as that is."

Zoe swayed on her feet. "I am, but it's also because you kept getting hurt during your fun little people-collection job, and all those other potions just weren't cutting it. But I experimented, and I gave you something that works especially well for you."

"What of it? This is why I hate a lot of this magic shit. It's all too complicated. I might not be able to build a gun from scratch, but at least I can tell you how it works."

"That's just it," Zoe said in a sing-song voice. "I don't even know why it works on you. Just be thankful that it does."

James threw open her door and stepped outside, then closed the door behind him and spared the house a final glance before heading to his truck. There was only so much drunken rambling a man could take, even from a sexy woman.

Later that night James pushed into the Leanan Sídhe, an

old moleskin notebook in hand. He spotted the Professor in a booth in the far back, and a woman with lush dark hair sat beside him. He took long strides until he arrived at the table.

The short woman looked up at him. She wore jeans and a black T-shirt, which hugged an athletic and toned body. She was a little younger than James, he estimated; probably in her upper twenties at most. Then again, for all he knew, she was two hundred and using magic to look younger.

Smite-Williams gestured to the empty seat across from him and James sat down. He took a good look the woman.

She smirked. "Like what you see, big man?"

James shrugged. "Just wondering who you are."

"Sure, pal." The woman rolled her eyes. "Keep telling yourself that."

James had no idea how to react, so he chose to ignore her. He opened his notebook and pulled a pen from his pocket.

In truth, given his photographic memory he didn't need notes, but he couldn't risk that some sort of injury or special magical attack might cost him that quality. The notebook represented a nice redundant intelligence source that he could always burn—and later reproduce—if he was in a dangerous situation.

The Professor cleared his throat. "James Brownstone, this is Shay Carson. I'll tell you her role in this once I explain the job."

James nodded. He trusted The Professor's judgment. Shay must obviously have some useful skills for her to even be sitting there.

"And before I can go into the job," the older man said, "I need to give you a little history lesson."

"My least-favorite subject," James muttered.

Shay snorted. "Why am I not surprised?"

The Professor glanced between them and shook his head. "Play nice, you two. You each provide complimentary skills for this job." He waved a hand. "Anyway, James, are you familiar with the Cartagena Codex?"

James searched his memory as he scribbled down the name. He was familiar enough with South American codices, particularly the Mayan folding books written on barkcloth. The Conquistadors had destroyed most of them, leaving a huge hole in pre-Colombian history. That said, he'd never heard of a Cartagena Codex.

The bounty hunter shook his head. "Nope."

Shay smirked, and the Professor shot her a harsh look. She shrugged but didn't say anything.

"It's a rather recent discovery," the Professor continued. "From what has been decoded, it was apparently written after the conquest of the Inca Empire by Pizzaro, by what may have been refugees who had resettled in a small surviving Mayan city."

"The Incas didn't have a full writing system, you see," Shay told him. "The Mayans did."

James shrugged. He knew that.

The Professor leaned forward, folding his hands in front of him. "The point is, lad, that unlike most other codices from the early periods, this one wasn't destroyed. It was transported from its city of origin and eventually ended up hidden in what is now Cartagena, Colombia. And it tells an interesting story."

"A *very* interesting story," Shay added.

James glanced at the woman. Nervous tension radiated from her, like she was desperate to prove something to him.

"A lot of what's in that codex might not have been believed twenty years ago," said Smite-Williams. "From what can be deciphered, it tells a story of Pizzaro gaining control of an ancient artifact, a rod that was supposed to be associated with the Inca god Supay, God of Death and the Underworld. His name is also associated with a race of demons, and the codex implies that Pizzaro actually made use of the artifact to summon dark creatures to aid him in fighting Inca forces."

"Bet they left that out of the reports back to Spain," James mumbled.

"You'll love what they were called," Shay added with a wink.

James shrugged. "All right, what were they called?"

"The closest translation would be 'corpse-demons that walk again.'"

"Goddamn motherfucking zombies," James spat. "Why does it have to be zombies?"

"Motherfucking zombies," Shay echoed.

"Aye, lad, zombies," the Professor agreed. He grinned. "Now, when you have your ear to the ground like I do, you hear a lot of things, and you can begin to piece disparate things together. Long story short, I have good information on the location of the Rod of Supay."

James took a deep breath and nodded. The good thing about taking down something like a zombie was that he wouldn't feel any guilt.

After all, they were already dead.

The Professor nodded toward Shay. "This is where Miss Carson comes in. She's a field archaeologist with good tactical skills. Considering the nature of this particular mission, that's a good combination."

"She's a graverobber who can use a gun," James joked.

"That or a kickass treasure hunter. I think the politically correct term is 'tomb raider.'" Shay smirked. "It's not always graves, you know. But I'm okay around weapons. Not like we live in a safe world."

"This time your skills will be particularly helpful, Miss Shay," the Professor said. "And convenient." He turned toward James. "We have a strong lead on the Rod that suggests it's buried in a tomb complex in northern Peru. It's been explored before, but we have reasons—many reasons, actually—to believe the Rod was magically shielded from detection, and there are no active excavations going on due to issues at the site and local rebel activity. Shay will be taking lead on this, and you'll be support."

"Unless you have a problem following a woman?" Shay asked, defiance in her eyes.

"Fine by me." James jotted down a few more notes and looked back up at the woman. The irritation on her face surprised him.

There was just one angle in this that hadn't been explored to his satisfaction. "That I'm being invited to the party implies this isn't just about digging up some moldy zombie rod. There's a bounty involved."

"Well, yes, James. Some others are interested in the Rod

of Supay" Smite-Williams said, his smile faltering for a moment.

"Who?"

"The *Brujos Rojos*."

James leaned back and nodded, trying not to let his disgust show. "I thought they got taken out when they tried to assassinate that high-ranking Light Elf during her visit to Colombia last year."

"Not enough of them were finished off. They've been recruiting, and now they're sniffing around the Rod of Supay. Whatever our various motivations for being interested in this artifact are, none of us wants a group of homicidal warlocks to get their hands on it."

James had tangled with the *Brujos Rojos*—the Red Warlocks—a few years before. They had a nasty little habit of kidnapping children from the Happy Magic Land Amusement Park in Anaheim to fuel spells.

They were the kind of men James had no problem destroying.

His hands curled into fists, and he gave the Professor a curt nod. "I'm in." He frowned as something occurred to him. "On one condition."

"What is that?" the older man asked, a curious glint in his eye. "Don't get greedy now, lad. You get to make money and kick some evil ass. Isn't that enough?"

James snorted. "My dog is missing. I'd like you to look for him while I'm on the job."

The Professor chuckled. "And here I thought you were going to ask for something much more expensive." He nodded at Shay. "Well, Miss Carson, it looks like you have support." He clapped his hands together. "And now, I do believe this is the part of the evening where Father O'Banion comes out to play."

Shay stretched languidly, her shirt riding up and exposing her toned abdomen for a moment. The peek caught James' attention, but he returned a second later to writing down a few more notes.

The treasure hunter scowled at him. James shrugged at her.

What was with this woman?

5

The Professor flagged down a waitress to ask for three Guinness Draughts. Or maybe it was more accurate to say that Father O'Banion ordered the drinks. Now that it was drinking time, Smite-Williams was ready to unleash his true drinking persona.

James didn't mind Father O'Banion most of the time—unless he sang. Then he was fucking insufferable. But he wasn't singing yet.

Hope still lived.

"Are all those for you?" James asked.

Father O'Banion frowned. "Of course not, lad. We need to toast future mutual and overlapping interests. Unless you're too good to toast with ol' Father O'Banion?"

Shay shot James a glance, confusion on her face.

"It's kind of a drinking thing," James explained. "Mostly harmless."

Father O'Banion shook his head. "Not 'kind of.' It's *totally* a drinking thing, and never harmless."

He grinned as the waitress returned with the three huge

glasses on her tray. She handed one to each person at the table before heading back to the bar.

The older man hefted his glass. "To defeating evil, acquiring knowledge, and making money—all at the same time."

"Here, here," Shay said, clinking her glass against his.

James only grunted before offering his glass.

Father O'Banion sucked down a good half of his drink in the blink of an eye. Even James was impressed, and he was used to the man's antics.

Shay sat quietly, her gaze roaming the bar and taking in every detail. Since James irritated her, from what he could tell, he decided to let her stew for a few minutes until she got some alcohol inside her. A little liquid relaxation never hurt anyone.

Once a more casual atmosphere had fully settled over the trio, James decided to try again with the prickly treasure hunter. He didn't need to know her well to work with her, but it wouldn't hurt.

James suspected she wouldn't want to talk about the finer points of barbeque, let alone the glories of Jessie Rae's God Sauce.

"So, you been doing field archaeology long?" James sipped some of his Guinness, enjoying the roasted barley flavor.

Shay narrowed her eyes. "Why do you want to know? You think I don't have what it takes?"

"Play nice, children," Father O'Banion ordered.

Her aggressive responses no longer surprised James.

"Nah, I know you have what it takes." He shrugged.

Shay's kneejerk reaction to almost everything made

James doubt that she'd been in a people-oriented job before taking up tomb raiding or graverobbing or whatever she wanted to call it. He resisted smirking at the thought.

The woman's face twisted in confusion. "You *know* I have what it takes, Brownstone?"

"Yeah, that's what I said, last time I checked."

The corner of Shay's mouth turned up. "And why are you so sure? You quick to trust, Brownstone? I would have thought a bounty hunter would be more cynical."

Father O'Banion let out a quiet chuckle at that, but didn't say anything. He was more interested in downing his Draught than getting in the way of Shay's verbal claws.

"Oh, I'm cynical as any other idiot out there," James replied, "but Father O'Banion wouldn't have recommended you if you weren't. I trust his judgment. I've worked with him a lot and he's never steered me wrong, which is more than I can say for a lot of people I've worked with."

The good Father finished his drink during this part of the conversation and exhaled loudly. "Aye, lad, but all this work talk is boring."

"What do you want to talk about, then?"

Father O'Banion tapped the side of his glass. "Let's sit here and get drunk and tell lies. Or is that tell lies until we're drunk? Either would be fine. Both are much more fun than talking about who's a cynical fuck."

James grinned. "Can't disagree with that."

Shay scoffed. "Takes all kinds."

James nodded. "That it does, but he's a lot like you."

"Not complaining too much. He's getting me this job, but what do you mean?"

"His appearance is deceiving."

Father O'Banion nodded gravely, a ridiculously serious look now fixed on his face.

Shay's eyes narrowed and she pursed her lips. "Oh, and you think you know me well enough to say that my appearance is deceiving, Brownstone?"

"Maybe."

The waitress returned with another Draught for Father O'Banion.

"You're doing the Lord's work, miss," O'Banion offered as the waitress departed.

Silence reigned for an uncomfortably long time after that. James didn't feel like saying anything else that might piss Shay off, and she seemed more interested in brooding and thinking up reasons to be offended.

Father O'Banion, of course, focused on the rapid consumption of copious amounts of booze.

Shay took a few more sips of her drink and finally spoke up. "Look, I know what I'm doing by freelancing with my archaeology skills."

James waved a hand in front of him. "Never said you didn't."

"We all need to make our money somehow, and there's a lot of good money in artifacts. Better I make some money and steer them into someone like Smite-Williams' hands."

"Again, not disagreeing," he replied.

James wondered why the woman was so hell-bent on trying to pick a fight with him. On some other night maybe he wouldn't have minded, but between having to deal with Zoe and his missing dog, he didn't need more stress.

"She's skilled, lad," Father O'Banion said, his face flushed and puffy. "*Very* skilled. More skilled than a lot of people with twice her experience. Kind of like you that way."

Shay nodded. "I'm fucking Lara Croft, just without all the money. Guess I'm doing this shit backward. Not all that interested in talking about my past, though, just in case you're the curious and nosey sort, Brownstone."

James set his glass down and nodded. No reason to press her for the moment. He still was earning her trust.

However slowly.

"I *can* be a curious and nosey sort, but I know when to leave well enough alone."

Father O'Banion snorted at that. "Some people and organizations may disagree."

"Yeah, what can I say? Results may vary. And I don't give a shit about Shay's past." James picked his glass back up to take another sip.

The lie would serve well enough. If Shay didn't want to talk about her past, she probably had a good reason. Maybe darkness and loss, like James' own. Maybe she just wasn't proud of the sort of work she'd done in the past.

It didn't matter. It wasn't really his business, and James knew all too well how the past could sink its claws into a person and refuse to let go, dragging them down to an abyss of personal suffering.

Father O'Banion stood. "I'll be right back. Need to make more room." Whistling, he got up and wandered toward the men's bathroom.

An awkward silence stretched between Shay and James.

"The past is shit," he offered.

Shay snickered. "The past is shit?"

"Yeah." James stared down into the dark liquid half-filling his glass. "That's what the last twenty years have taught everybody, I figure. If they haven't learned that lesson, they are dumbasses."

Shay nodded slowly. "I get it. I mean, we all grew up reading about history and science, and what could happen and couldn't—and then we find out it's all bullshit, and that magic is real. In a sense, everything we've known...the truths humanity's known and told each other for thousands of years were all lies."

"Makes you wonder what that means for the future. There's still so much we don't know about Oriceran, and it's changing everything over here. I see it every day on my job. Fuck, that's why every country needs bounty hunters like me now."

James slowly exhaled, lost in the thoughts of the kinds of magic he'd witnessed and used, let alone the dangerous things he had locked up at his house. Minor differences like whether a person had grown up with the internet seemed like nothing compared to whether a person had grown up knowing magic was real. "Take the pyramids, for instance," he offered. "Big-ass tombs for long-dead pharaohs? Not even fucking close."

He shrugged. "Well, okay, some were, but most of them were energy machines built by real Atlanteans hell-bent on maintaining power over twenty-fucking-thousand years ago. All that bullshit about how many years mankind has been smart?" He tapped his head. "Makes no damned sense when we have stone villages under the water in the Mediterranean Sea that are a lot older. And that lie was being questioned *before* the Oricerans showed up. Makes you wonder who was hiding the truth in plain fucking sight for so long, and why."

"You truly are a world-class cynic."

"I am," he agreed.

Shay tapped her fingers against the table. "Who knew?"

"Who knew what?"

"That you actually had something interesting to say, Brownstone. I kind of pegged you just as a give-a-punch-and-take-a-punch guy. That, and a grunter."

James shrugged and raised his eyebrows. "I'm all that, too." He grunted.

Shay chuckled.

James almost laughed. They'd managed to have a half-way decent conversation without Shay shooting him a nasty look.

Maybe the job wouldn't be so bad after all.

Father O'Banion emerged from the bathroom, smiling more widely than before. He walked over to the table just in time for the waitress to deliver him a new Draught.

"Thank you, miss," he told her, picking up his new glass. He nodded toward the other side of the bar and asked his tablemates, "Someone I knew came in when I was doing my business. Mind if I join them for a bit?"

James shrugged. "Knock yourself out."

"I don't care," Shay offered.

Father O'Banion gave them a little salute. "I'll be back in a few minutes."

Once he'd crossed the room, Shay frowned at her empty glass. "So, Smite-Williams gets a new drink automatically, and I don't? That's some sexist bullshit."

This time James did laugh. "I think it's more that he practically lives here, and they know to keep them coming.

"Maybe," Shay grumbled.

"You really think the waitress is discriminating against you?"

"I don't know." Shay pushed off the table to stand. "I'm gonna go get a drink. Be right back."

Shay forced a smile onto her face as she walked away from the table. She'd seen Brownstone checking her out, but the guy kept acting like he didn't care. Brownstone did care. He *had* to. All men cared about hot women. They couldn't help it. That was the way they were wired. That was how most men were, really—a dick tangentially connected to a pair of eyes, totally bypassing the brain.

Shay wasn't into pretending she wasn't hot as fucking sin.

Sometimes that could be an advantage when trying to manipulate men, but it didn't mean she had to like it when men leered at her. She wasn't a fucking piece of meat to sate their damned hunger.

Brownstone was no different. Just because he could play it cool didn't mean he wasn't thinking about her. She'd prove it yet.

Her pace slowed at a sudden thought. *Unless he was gay.*

Shay tossed the possibility around in her head. That would explain why he wasn't drooling over her. The old man was one thing, but Brownstone was close to her age. It just didn't make sense otherwise.

She nodded to herself, satisfied that she now had a good initial hypothesis about what made James Brownstone tick.

Poor guy, they were in the wrong kind of bar for him. Maybe she was getting ahead of herself, but she liked the idea, the more she thought about it.

A couple of drunk yahoos in suits eyed her from a table, their gazes roaming up and down her body and lingering on all the best places.

Fuckers. Her body was all they saw, and all they cared about.

One of the suits decided to get brave. Stupid, but brave. He reached for her ass.

Shay snapped out with a lightning-fast kick. The other man didn't even have time to register what was going before his grabby-hands friend flew to the ground, head smashing against the tile. His wooden chair clattered against the floor.

Every conversation in the bar stopped, and every patron looked her way.

The suit yahoo moaned and held his head. His friend rushed out of his chair and crouched beside him.

The angry woman lowered her leg. "Don't grab my ass and you won't get kicked. Pretty simple, asshole."

The moaner's friend helped lift him, and they fled out the door into the night.

What a bunch of chickenshits. Not that Shay was looking for a barroom brawl. Not that she *wasn't* looking for one, either.

Shay sauntered to the bar, daring anyone to say shit about what she'd just done. "I can't believe how crap the service is here if you're a woman," she muttered under her breath.

"Was that really necessary?" the bartender asked.

"'Necessary' is a relative thing. And I bet you he doesn't grab some woman's ass any time soon."

The bartender nodded. "Can't say you're wrong there."

Shay pinned the bartender with her glare. "Need a refill on my Draught."

The beer wasn't her favorite, but she liked the buzz settling into her head, so she might as well continue with what was working.

The bartender poured her a new glass.

"Thanks." She grabbed it and headed back to her table.

Light conversation had picked up around the bar again. Shay snickered, wondering if someone getting their ass kicked was a common occurrence at the Leanan Sídhe. She'd been told about some dog that drank from a bottle, but he wasn't there that night. That would have been a sight.

Brownstone watched her, but held no annoyance in his eyes. If anything, Shay would have said he looked amused.

Shay dropped back into her seat, setting her glass in front of her. "Got something to say?"

"Nope."

"Is that gonna be a problem for you or Smite-Williams?"

James laughed. "You'll have to kick a lot more ass before you catch up to the number of people he's beat up in this bar."

Shay grinned at that. She was liking the old drunk more and more.

Something about the situation still bothered her, though, and it took a few more seconds of thinking to figure it out.

She'd appreciated that Brownstone hadn't jumped up to defend her, since it meant he respected her skills. She might need his help against some kid-snatching warlocks in Peru, but a few idiots in a bar were fine.

At the same time, Shay didn't like the idea the guy hadn't at least tried to be a gentleman.

"You let guys grab women's asses in here, Brownstone?"

"Do you think I should have done something about that? Do you think I even had time to?"

James stared at Shay until she grimaced and looked away.

"Just saying, is all," she muttered.

James looked over at the table where the drunk suited yahoos had been sitting. "If you need my help, you'll get it. If you don't need it, you won't get it. It's a waste of time otherwise."

"And your time's that valuable, Brownstone?"

He grunted, a small smile playing on his lips. "Yeah, that's why I get the big bucks."

Shay watched him for a moment before shaking her head and focusing on her drink. Maybe Brownstone was gay, maybe he wasn't. He might be a gentleman, or a first-rate ass. She just didn't know what to think of the guy.

That, more than anything, made her uneasy.

6

Shay eyed the tiny rickety prop plane, wondering if she and James would die on their way to rather than at or back from the tomb in northern Peru.

The first leg of their trip, which took them to Tapachula, Mexico, had been pleasant enough if a little boring, but at least they had been in a jet and not something that looked like it had been found in some old aviation museum.

The pilot waved from beside the plane. The man's cheerful energy was infectious, but with his leathery skin he resembled a mummy more than a living person.

Shay couldn't estimate his age. He might just have spent a few extra years working the fields, or he might be ready to stroke out the minute they hit turbulence.

"Jesus," Shay muttered. It wouldn't be her worst bit of travel since starting her career in freelance archaeology, but it might be a contender.

James took a good look at the plane while he adjusted the straps on his backpack. "The Professor guarantees this guy. He knows a lot of places where we can land and take off without attracting too much attention."

"Like the oceans or the tops of the mountains?" Shay grinned. "Whatever. I'm going to sleep the whole time, so if we crash it'll be over before I even know what's going on."

They started toward the plane.

James cleared his throat. "They might not be there, you know."

Shay glanced at him. "Who?"

"The *Brujos Rojos*."

"That'd be great, but I doubt we'll get so lucky."

"I'll deal with anyone who needs to be dealt with," James rumbled. "More bounties, more money."

Shay eyed the man for a second, wondering if he believed she'd never killed anyone. They didn't need to get into that, so she didn't bother to offer up her thoughts on the subject.

Some shit needed to remain private.

They closed on the plane now, and a side hatch lay open. The pilot leaned against the plane, his arms crossed.

"*Hola!*" the pilot called. "Neither of you gringos get sick in planes, do you? Gonna be a long trip."

They'd made it.

The jeep rumbled down the dirt track, bouncing and shaking the entire time. While they didn't have the luxury of taking a true road to the dig site, they'd managed to find an abandoned logging path that would get them close.

After so many hours on a cramped plane, a few hours in a jeep driving through rough terrain felt like heaven.

Shay didn't care, as long as they got to the site. Finding the Rod of Supay would make her a lot more money, and burnish her tomb-raiding reputation.

Colorful plants and animals passed in a blur, mostly ignored by the treasure hunter and the bounty hunter. They were more concerned about their mission than sightseeing.

James stared into the jungle as if he expected the warlocks to burst through the brush at any second.

Shit, for all Shay knew they would. Her focus wasn't on fighting and hunting every crazed rogue magical group out there. That was why she'd brought the big guy.

James had barely spoken since they'd gotten into the jeep, not that he'd spoken a lot before that. The guy liked to deliver a few smart-ass remarks, then retreat into watchful silence.

Being this close together only reinforced in her mind that James was probably gay. He was damned fussy with his equipment and his weapons. Plus, the bastard hadn't made one move on her the entire time.

"You know, Brownstone, you could talk."

"I don't know how," James joked. "Sometimes I forget."

"This might end up being pretty boring and not profitable for you if your boys don't show up."

James peered into the jungle ahead. "Oh, they'll show up."

"How can you be so sure?"

"The bait's too great, and the Professor wouldn't have

bothered asking me to come if he didn't think you needed me."

"That's a comforting thought."

James grinned. "Well, I'm not here to make you feel better. I'm here to take out any bastards that bother us."

Shay slowed the jeep when what looked like a large mound in the distance caught her eye. "Looks like we're almost there."

The only problem was the trees thickening ahead of them. Where was a clear-cut when you needed it?

They both fell back into silence and searched the area for any signs of recent passage. From what James had told Shay on the first leg of their plane trip the Red Warlocks specialized in blood magic, so at least they wouldn't have to worry about a fireball exploding over them out of nowhere.

Shay frowned and brought the jeep to a stop.

"We'll have to hoof it from here. Too bad. A few miles in the jungle isn't a recreational hike." She sighed.

James moved his head back and forth, popping his neck. "Then we'd better get going."

The trip through the jungle went faster than James expected, and they now stood in front of a crumbling stone archway and weathered stairs leading into inky darkness below. Torn small flags and the occasional discarded tool hinted at the last group of explorers.

"At least we didn't have to do a lot of climbing," Shay said, linking her fingers and stretching her arms above her.

She followed that by double-checking her holster, her machete sheath, and her knife sheath.

"Sure."

James could appreciate her attention to murderous detail. Even the most powerful warlock couldn't do shit if you got the drop on him and blew his brains out—not to mention cutting off his head.

The noise of the jungle surrounded them: the flutter of birds' wings, buzzing of insects, the shuffling of God-knew-what. A powerful and evil magical artifact might lie inside this ancient tomb.

Evil energy had a way of attracting evil.

The sound of running water in the distance reached the bounty hunter's ears and he stopped for a moment, thinking about the map they'd studied. He didn't need to bring out a device to check.

The tomb site lay atop a tall cliff, with a river snaking past well below it. The site was inaccessible from that side because of the difficulty of scaling a cliff in the middle of dense jungle, but in an emergency they could probably climb down and follow the river.

They approached the stone arch, and after exchanging glances, they pulled out their flashlights and turned them on. The beams cut into the darkness, revealing nothing but stairs descending to a dusty chamber below.

"Let's do this," Shay exclaimed.

James gave her a nod.

Their footsteps echoed in the eerie silence until they arrived at the bottom of the stairs, where smaller tunnels proceeded off in three directions. Their equal spacing around the room made them hard to differentiate. Shay could see how a person could easily get disoriented in the chamber.

Not that it bothered her. She'd paid close attention to her angle as they entered the chamber, and she knew exactly where to go.

The treasure hunter pointed to her left. "That leads to the main burial chamber. Given the small size of this place, I think it'll be easy to find the rod." She stepped toward the tunnel.

"Glad *some* things in life are easy," James replied.

Shay grinned. "This place has mostly been excavated already, so we don't have to worry about traps or anything until we get near the main burial chamber." She grinned, a sinister visage given that her face was cloaked in the shadows of the tomb.

Excitement swelled in Shay.

For all the talk of the creepy warlocks, she would be able to snag the artifact without much trouble in the end. Getting a payday would be sweet enough, but being able to do it without breaking a sweat?

That was a big-assed bonus.

Shay chuckled to herself, thinking about James as their footsteps echoed and mingled in the narrow passageway. Even though the gay bounty hunter insisted that he had nothing but respect for her skill, he probably still carried some doubts. Recovering this artifact would prove to him that she had what it took, and then…

Then what? Shay furrowed her brow. It wasn't like the man was going to eat his words. He'd already said that he trusted in her skills. She gritted her teeth. It was frustrating when she was ready for a fight but the other person wouldn't play.

James continued to walk beside her in silence, step after step. The sound was almost hypnotic when she focused on it.

It took her a few moments to accept what she was hearing: a strange buzzing that had not been there before. She was sure of it.

In any other place, the slightest background noise would have swallowed the buzzing. Birds tweeting or the slight rustle of the wind would have been more than enough to mask it, but there in the shadows of the tomb with nothing but the eternal silence of death, the quiet sound stood out as if someone were screaming.

Shay's heartrate kicked up and she froze in place, then slowly turned around, her hand dropping to the holster. Taking a deep breath, she pulled her weapon out.

James had already drawn his pistol. "You heard it, too. I'm impressed," he whispered.

Shay smirked despite the situation and peered into the darkness, holding her flashlight arm under her pistol arm to help better steady both. Her beam joined the bounty hunter's in piercing the darkness.

It didn't take long to find another anomaly. Her beam caught a faint shimmer near the entrance, just past where they'd entered the tunnel. Her partner's beam caught something that made her hiss.

James had changed his angle toward the floor while Shay lighted the shimmer. Bloody footsteps marred the floor.

The shimmer vanished, and three men in scarlet robes winked into sight.

"If you leave now," one of them said, "you won't die. You cannot defeat the *Brujos Rojos*. Your greed has brought you to your doom."

"Okay, guess that confirms that they're bad guys," Shay mumbled.

James holstered his pistol. "Yeah, I'd worry a lot more about your own doom there, assholes."

"What the hell are you doing?" Shay whispered. "Are you planning to talk them into submission?"

James chuckled. "If only that would work." The bounty hunter shook his head, although he kept his gaze locked on the three men. "I've dealt with the *Brujos Rojos* before," he whispered. "They like to get close. If they can get a good cut on you, their blood magic is fucking vicious."

"Isn't that more of a reason to shoot them from very far away?"

"Nope." He shrugged. "Go ahead and take a shot."

Shay frowned. The men's threat had made their identity clear, and even if they were willing to let the field archaeologist and her support go, they'd get control of the zombie rod. She wasn't about to lose her payday and let some asshole warlocks get a free artifact. She pulled the trigger.

One of them men jerked, and Shay grinned. She had plenty of confidence in her weapons skills, but it was satisfying to see a bad guy go down.

Except that he didn't. The struck warlock remained silent as he dropped his robe to the ground as if in challenge, pointing to a huge wound on his shoulder. Even though his face was contorted in pain, the flesh was already repairing itself.

"Something about soul proximity or some shit," James said. "Overly complicated crap. All I know is that they are dangerous up close, but they are also weak up close. And if they are out cold, their magic is worthless."

The bounty hunter sprang at them suddenly, surprising Shay, and from the startled jumps of the warlocks, he surprised them as well. Their fingernails grew into glistening claws, but the charging bounty hunter had already closed the gap.

He slammed a fist into the head of the closest warlock, and his victim crashed into a wall with an echoing thud before falling to the hard stone paving the floor of the tunnel. Taking advantage of his momentum, James continued his assault by landing a spinning kick square on the chest of a second warlock. The guy smashed headfirst into the tunnel wall opposite the first victim.

He grinned. Beating down child-snatching warlocks was damn satisfying.

Two down, one to go. The remaining warlock was Shay's bullet sponge from before.

His wound had already sealed itself.

The bastard offered James a sickening grin. He'd taken the time to cast a spell while his friends were getting the beat-down. A bloody film now covered the warlock's eyes, and they glowed with a soft crimson light.

His newly-grown claws dripped dark liquid.

Shay slammed her pistol into her holster and sheathed her knife. She didn't want to let Brownstone show her up, but she didn't have to be an expert mage to recognize that the warlock now had poison-tipped claws. The power of blood magic couldn't be easily dismissed.

James stared at the man for a second before shaking his head. "Still not too late to surrender, asshole."

Apparently the power of blood magic was easily dismissed if you were an Angeleno bounty hunter.

The warlock yelled and slashed at James, and he grabbed the guy's arms and yanked hard to either side, dislocating both the man's shoulders. A blood-curdling scream filled the chamber. James finished by headbutting the warlock's face, and the man's nose crunched and his eyes rolled up. James let go, and the unconscious man fell to the ground.

Shay caught up to James. "Okay then, Brownstone, I'll admit it. You've got skills."

James pointed with his thumb at the other end of the tunnel. "You go get the Rod. I'll deal with these jokers."

Shay nodded and jogged back the way she'd come, her heart still racing from the short fight. She'd not expected that the warlocks would be too much trouble, but she'd also expected they would have been at least a *little* bit of a problem. James' presence had been a great help, even if she didn't want to stress that to him.

The tunnel gave way to an octagonal room. A large stone sarcophagus dominated the center, its lid already removed by the previous expedition and its occupant also gone.

Shay didn't care, since she wasn't there for a dead Inca. She was there for a rod that made dead people walk. She circled the chamber, carefully pointing her flashlight at the junctures where the walls met the floor. Her research had suggested there was a hidden area in the room.

A couple of minutes' effort rewarded her search, although she would have missed it if she hadn't known exactly what she was looking for: a small carving in the wall that when looked at from a certain angle and illuminated with only a single beam of light resembled a stylized humanoid figure.

The earlier expedition might have eventually found it if they'd not had to worry about things like Communist insurgents. Shay snickered to herself. When she'd taken the job, she'd not been worried about the idea they might run into local rebels. Brownstone didn't seem to care either. The only real threat were the warlocks.

Of course, even if the earlier expedition hadn't fled, they wouldn't have found what she sought. From what the Professor had told her, the magical shielding of the site had concealed hidden treasure chambers like the one she was about to open.

There was probably gold and jewelry to be found, but she didn't care. The payoff from the Rod alone would make the trip worthwhile, and she didn't want to stick around in case more warlocks showed up. Handling thirty might not be as easy as handling three.

Even if the expedition had found the spot on the wall, she doubted they would have been able to figure what to do next. Being a "field archaeologist," whether you wanted to call someone in that profession a treasure hunter or tomb raider, required equal parts daring and knowledge.

"Blood freely given will reveal the sacred treasure," Shay recalled. She grabbed her knife and sliced the tip of one of her fingers. Rubbing her hand over the carving, she grinned to herself.

I'm damn good.

The burial chamber rumbled, and Shay straightened, crossing her arms and waiting. The wall parted on the other side, revealing a small stone box and a faded wall painting of a dark-eyed man in a dark cloak wearing a round golden headpiece. She'd seen similar depictions in her research for the job.

It was undoubtedly Supay.

Shay spent a minute to search around the box for any indications of a trap. Satisfied that she wasn't about to be blown up or poisoned, she pushed the lid off, releasing a cloud of dust.

A curved bone rod lay inside. Swirling patterns and sigils that Shay didn't recognize decorated the artifact.

Not taking any chances, Shay slipped some gloves on before grabbing the Rod of Supay. Fortunately, from everything she'd read, it didn't activate without exposure to blood. She slipped the covered rod into her backpack and took a deep breath.

"That went well," Shay murmured to herself.

She had to admit that if she'd been by herself, she might have misjudged the warlocks, but that didn't mean they would have won. It wasn't that she *needed* Brownstone.

He'd just made things easier.

With the Rod of Supay in hand, Shay didn't see any reason to stick around. She walked out of the burial chamber and headed into the tunnel. James was gone, as were the downed warlocks. Picking up the pace, Shay hurried out of the tunnel into the entrance chamber and up the stairs.

James stood at the top, an unconscious and zip-tied warlock lying next to him.

Shay patted her backpack. "I got it."

"Good."

She glanced down at the warlock. "What happened to the other two guys? When we were flying down here, I thought you told me that you could get a bounty per guy."

James shrugged. "No room on the plane. I should have thought that through." He pointed his thumb over his shoulder. "So I threw the other two into the river. Hope the alligators don't get indigestion."

Shay stared at him for a moment. He looked bored, and she had no idea if he was telling the truth. For all she knew, he had eaten them for magical power.

They needed to get out of there, so she decided to roll with it.

"You have a very dry sense of humor, Mr. Brownstone," Shay told him. "Let's get the hell out of here."

7

Shay let out a huge yawn as she stepped into the Leanan Sídhe, briefcase in hand. The carefully-wrapped Rod of Supay rested inside. The Professor's insistence on doing the hand-off at the bar surprised her, but the guy paying the bill got to make the call. After she gave him the Rod, it wasn't her business what happened to the Inca zombie-maker.

Not that the possibility troubled her much. Shay doubted someone like Smite-Williams would sell it to some murderous-dictator asshole. Granted, the next world war probably would involve crazy shit like armies of zombies and demons.

That was just reality now.

The bartender shot Shay a faint frown as she stepped in and closed the door behind her. She recognized him from the night she'd made an example of Mr. Grabby Hands. If he wasn't going to throw her out, she didn't give a crap how irritated he was. Besides, if no one touched her, she wouldn't have to beat them down. So really, he should have been mad at Mr. Grabby Hands for setting her off.

A few men near the entrance watched her with hungry eyes, and she updated the forecast to a thirty-percent chance of ass-kicking. It wasn't her fault men couldn't think with their brains instead of their dicks, and it also wasn't her fault she was hot.

The Professor waved cheerfully from a table near the back, a half-empty mug in front of him. Father O'Banion must have been eager to come out that night.

Shay lingered near the entrance to survey the bar for possible threats. The clientele varied: business jerks, college kids, bored-looking couples, and a group of old ladies in red hats dominating several tables in the center. No one paid her much attention other than the leer patrol, and there were no signs of subtle tension on anyone's face.

If there were any troublemakers in there they weren't looking for her, or they were damn good at hiding it. Few people could pull that off, even professionals. That desire to harm—that killer instinct—blazed like a flare at midnight if a person knew how to look for it.

Now more comfortable, Shay sauntered to the Professor's table. No one risked their limbs by trying to cop a feel this time, and some of her tension drifted away.

Shay set the briefcase down before taking a seat. "Hey."

The Professor offered her a polite nod. "Good evening, Miss Carson."

Shay frowned, realizing there was one man she hadn't seen during her survey of the bar.

"Where's Brownstone? He better not be off polishing his guns or something stupid like that."

"Ah, the fine lad is at the police station turning in his bounty. Such good money in bringing in rogue warlocks, especially nasty ones." The Professor clucked his tongue. "It's a shame he couldn't bring them all in, but at least three troublemakers won't be a problem anymore, one way or another." He followed the statement with a grin.

"I'm not losing any sleep over those assholes." Shay patted the briefcase, then slid it over. "Your gift from our *vacation*. The lock is genetically sealed to you."

"Oh! It's like my birthday and Christmas all rolled into one." The Professor pressed his thumb on a small pad near the lock, and there was a slight burning sensation. He lifted his now-smooth thumb and shook it out. The DNA sampler had taken the top layer of skin.

Thirty seconds passed before the lock finally clicked. He pulled open the lid, and his smile faded.

"Problem?" Shay asked, tensing.

During all her dealings with Smite-Williams, the man had worn a near-constant grin. If anything he was *too* happy, and it annoyed her that the man didn't seem to be faking it.

Pissy rudeness made the world go around. A smart person always watched their back more near a smiling guy than a glaring asshole.

Probably much of his happy manner had to do with him drinking half the state's beer supply each night, but that didn't change the fact that seeing him look serious for once unsettled Shay. She also didn't want a guy she halfway liked to try to screw her out of the rest of her money.

"No problem at all, Miss Carson. It's just that no matter how many years I've been doing this, whenever I get my hands on one of these things I'm reminded of how many casual dangers now rest in the world. Especially those artifacts that might not have been so much of a threat even twenty years ago." He shook his head. "Kind of makes the threats of nuclear war that I grew up with almost seem quaint. At least we *understood* the nature of the danger."

Shay didn't like the path of the conversation. The last thing she wanted to deal with was a morose drunk—not to mention she didn't care.

Newsflash: the world sucked ass, and always had. Shay didn't give a shit. She only cared about getting paid.

"I know. Dangerous world, blah, blah." The treasure hunter smirked. "It also makes this job a lot more profitable, so at least there's an upside for me."

The Professor raised an eyebrow.

Shay shrugged. "Hope my greed doesn't bother you too much."

Smite-Williams' smile returned. "A knife is useful, regardless of whether it cares what it's cutting."

"You stay up all night thinking of that one?" Shay scoffed.

"Maybe I have a lot of them saved up after so many years. With age comes wisdom, or at least more bullshit."

Shay snickered.

The Professor reached into the suitcase, grabbed a pair of gloves already inside, and slipped them on. He carefully reached back inside the case and retrieved the Rod of Supay.

The bone rod looked different in the light of the Irish pub; less sinister, somehow. Shay didn't know if that was her mind playing tricks or if the Rod was less powerful away from its homeland, but she wanted it gone and to receive her money soon either way.

"The natural order's a curious thing," the Professor said. "Maybe we've been incorrect in what we included in that natural order, but it doesn't matter how much the world has changed. Some things shouldn't exist." He pushed the Rod back into the bag, slammed the briefcase shut, and chugged down more beer. "This is good beer. You should have some."

Shay sighed. This was taking longer than she wanted. "Not to be rude, but what about the rest of my payment?"

"Aye, of course. This old soul rambles on at times." Smite-Williams winked and pulled his phone out of his pocket and tapped furiously for a few moments. "That should do it."

Shay's phone dinged, and she glanced at the screen. Her gaze flicked up to her temporary employer. "It's a little more than you promised."

"James spoke about your efficiency and bravery." The Professor shrugged. "I like to cultivate the right sort of friends, Miss Carson. I think that's a good thing. Don't you?"

"Sure, that's a good thing. If we're friends now, how about helping your friend out with another job?"

The Professor chuckled. "Eager, are we?"

"Reap in the time of plenty so you don't starve in the time of famine."

Shay suppressed a shiver. She'd learned the line from an old employer, one much less pleasant than Smite-Williams.

"A poet's soul in you, Miss Carson?"

Shay's patience grew thin. "Do you have any other jobs or not?"

Smite-William locked eyes with her for a moment, then a soft smile settled on his face. "Aye, there's something else in the works. I'll let you know when I have more details."

"Thanks."

The red-faced man lifted his mug, toasting in her direction before downing the rest of his glass. He sighed. "Now that business is done, want to join me for a few more drinks? Or a lot more drinks?"

Business was definitely finished. She knew what was coming next, and amusing as it might be, she had other things to take care of that night.

"Sorry, Father O'Banion," Shay said with grin. "I have a few things to check on. Maybe next time." She rose and turned to leave.

"Your loss, Miss Carson. Your loss. We're having a contest tonight. A special singing contest."

Shay gave him a wave over her shoulder and headed toward the door.

An hour and many drinks later, Father O'Banion's prayers to Saint Cecilia were answered. With the briefcase stored in a sealed and protected safe in the back, he didn't have to worry about anything other than challenging his liver. The damn little bastard had been getting cheeky in recent years, not letting him get drunk as quickly as he wanted.

They called it "alcohol tolerance." He called it annoying.

Gulping down another Harp Lager, Father O'Banion

thought back to his meeting with Shay. When he'd come across her name he'd been unsure if she was the right choice for the job, which was one of the reasons he needed a man as reliable as James as support. But the pair had executed the mission with precision and speed.

He didn't care about her professed motivations. An evil artifact was out of circulation, and a few evil bastards would no longer trouble the world. It was nice work for the good guys, or at least the not-total-bastard guys.

The treasure hunter intrigued Father O'Banion. The rumors he'd heard of her past hadn't suggested a woman who would be a good fit as one of his associates, even as morally flexible as he was sometimes. Then again, many people might say the same thing about James, and there was truly a man pushing back the darkness.

For the moment, Father O'Banion could forget all about evil artifacts and tomb raiders. More beers awaited his attention, and even more important, his adoring public needed to be treated to the finest drunken singing in all of Los Angeles. No, the finest in the United States.

"Show us what you got, Father O'Banion," a man yelled from the bar. "Bill's last song was fucking great. I almost pissed myself. You better make me piss myself."

Father O'Banion stood and offered his fellow alcohol lovers an exaggerated bow. There was no way he'd let his championship title be taken. Losing his Bard of Filth plaque would be as bad as losing his manhood. He opened his mouth and let his inner drunk-ass idol free.

"I dream of a land where men can find what they need,
"Like beautiful women with their massive jugs freed."

Several men whooped and hollered.

Father O'Banion stopped and grinned. "I was talking about milk jugs, you dirty bastards."

Everyone shared a laugh as he continued.

Now what's a good rhyme for penis?

James sat in the creaky plastic chair waiting for the on-duty bounty processing sergeant, Mack, to call him up. Cops, civilians, and criminals flowed around him, and the overlapping conversations created a din. A police station was a microcosm of the best and worst humanity had to offer: the shields of the innocent and the vicious parasites pretending to be people.

Magic returning to the world hadn't changed anything about that. All it'd done was make things worse. Now even the stupidest-ass criminal could stumble onto something powerful. Chaos hadn't swallowed the world yet, but there were no guarantees for the future.

"Brownstone," Sergeant Mack bellowed from the front. "Get your ass up here."

James stood, grabbing a large unmarked box of donuts he'd brought with him. He marched to the front counter, behind which the huge bald black sergeant eyed him with a frown like James'd pissed in his coffee that morning.

A grin threatened to form at the thought.

James didn't know Mack's age. The cop hadn't presented a new wrinkle in all the years the bounty hunter had been coming to the station. Mack was also one of the few men James dealt with who had a lower voice than he did. There was something almost comforting about hearing him speak.

The cop's face cracked into a smile. "It's all been processed, Brownstone. Your payment's been made to the usual account, and a bonus will be coming in forty-eight hours because you nailed a high-priority target." Mack whistled. "*Brujos Rojos*? You caught one bad sonofabitch this time."

James decided to not mention that he'd disposed of the other two. He doubted Sergeant Mack would mind, but oversharing probably wouldn't help him. *KISS*.

James shrugged. "A bounty's a bounty. No big deal."

"Yeah, child-snatching blood-magic-using warlocks are totally the same thing as some Orci dusthead who skipped out on bail." The sergeant shook his head and tapped away at the computer on the counter in front of him. "And aren't you working too hard, man? What…twelve bounties last month weren't enough for you? Shit, and most of those were above Level Three."

Two patrol officers walked by and gave James a polite nod. "Keep up the good work, Brownstone."

James grunted in response and glanced down at the box of donuts, waiting for the right time to offer his gift.

One of cops clapped him on the shoulder before they headed off.

"Damn, Brownstone." Mack let out a low chuckle. "I was just looking at your stats for the last year. You're a fucking justice department in a leather jacket. I'm thinking that if you keep this up, they are gonna close down the department and I'm gonna lose my job. Streets will be too damn safe to justify having police." He grinned. "Think of my kids, Brownstone. Leave some criminals for us poor cops."

James shook his head. "I'm not doing much. I'm just a bounty hunter, not law enforcement. You guys are the real heroes."

Sergeant Mack shrugged. "Not that I'm disagreeing, but don't sell yourself short, Brownstone."

"I get to pick and choose which asshole I want to go after, and I don't have to pretend to be nice about it. You guys are out there every day, risking your lives and having to treat a lot of those pieces of shit nicely." James set the box on the counter. "It's not much, but at least it's something. Two dozen from Voodoo. I got different kinds."

Sergeant Mack carefully opened the box as if it contained a magical treasure. "That's mighty nice of you, Brownstone. I appreciate it, and the rest of the guys will appreciate it too. Thanks." The sergeant furrowed his brow. "Hey, did you see *Barbecue Wars* this week?"

James shook his head. "Don't tell me anything. Getting that bounty took me out of town, and I'm not caught up yet."

"Okay, okay. They mentioned your favorite place."

"Jessie Rae's?"

"Yep."

James chuckled and nodded. "Thanks for letting me know. See you later."

He respected the police, but that didn't mean he was comfortable hanging out around the station jaw-jacking all night. Plus, the Professor hadn't picked up any rumors about Leeroy, and Alison hadn't spotted any sign of the black lab either. Leeroy needed James, and the bounty hunter intended to find his best friend.

"Brownstone," Mack called to him.

James stopped and looked over his shoulder. "What?"

"Just a lot of chatter on the street about you pissing people off more than usual. Normally I'd say that's just you doing your job, but some of these guys are seriously bad dudes."

"What can I say? I'm really lovable—like a five-foot-eleven teddy bear."

The sergeant shook his head. "Just be careful out there, Brownstone."

"You should be telling that to the criminals on my list." James pushed open the doors and stepped out of the room.

8

James yawned as he stepped out of his F-350. He didn't mind foreign bounties, but traveling the fucking world was annoying. It'd been a while since he'd had to leave the United States, and he'd forgotten how exhausting it could be. Too bad he hadn't brought Zoe's energy potion with him.

At least I didn't use it. That means I don't have go back and see the horny Lush Queen anytime soon.

He wondered for a second what Zoe's personality would be like if she weren't drunk. He yawned again.

A faint grin split his face. He didn't need any magical enhancement to fight warlocks, but he did need them to deal with flying. That would hurt his reputation if it got out.

He could see it now. *Hey, the Granite Ghost needs a nap because he was on a plane too long. Bring the baby his bottle.*

James headed toward his door. Home sweet home. Now that he was back, he could spend a few days concentrating on finding Leeroy. He didn't get why it was so difficult to find him this time. The black lab liked to wander, but usually he didn't stray far.

Maybe Leeroy had found himself some bitch to shack up with. That was what James got for not getting him fixed. He just couldn't bring himself to do it to his best friend.

All the humor drained from the bounty hunter, and his eyes narrowed. Light from the inside leaked out, because his door was open. There was no fucking way he'd left it unlocked. Also, the alarm system wouldn't have activated with an open door. For that matter, he'd turned off his lights when he left.

James whipped out his .45 and pushed the door open with his foot. He stepped inside his house, gun raised, listening and watching for any movement. Only the ticks of wall clocks reached his ear.

A quick check of the alarm panel near the door revealed the system was powered off.

James' alarm didn't call the cops. It called someone scarier: him. But he'd checked it several times during the job to confirm no movement in his home. He'd not been worried about burglars; he'd been looking for evidence that Leeroy had returned home.

The house's motion sensors were calibrated to not set off the alarm when they detected something dog-sized, but they still would record the movement in the system log.

James kept his gun up as he pulled out his phone to check his alarm status. According to the control app the alarm was still active, which meant whoever had broken into his house wasn't some garden-variety punk. They had the skills to spoof the alarm signal. The tech wasn't exactly

NSA-quality, but it wasn't some shitty gear he'd grabbed from a guy downtown either.

Some fuckers needed to learn respect. He let a lot of shit slide, but invading his home was definitely on his "get your head kicked into your ass" list. James pocketed his phone and grunted.

He continued with his sweep. There were no threats in the hallway, bathroom, or living room.

"What the fuck?"

His irritation flared into incandescent rage as James stepped into the dining room. His heart thundered, and he let out a low growl.

Leeroy—but not Leeroy.

"I...will...fucking...kill...you...all," he ground out, each word thunder to the lightning his eyes threatened to fling.

His black lab lay butchered on a large silver serving tray in the dining room. James trembled with rage as he stepped forward. His gaze focused on a series of kanji characters on the plate. He recognized them immediately: Harriken.

Fucking animals. The bastard gangsters had murdered his dog and had the fucking balls to all but leave a goddamn signed confession.

James slipped his pistol back into his holster and took several deep breaths. He hadn't cried since he was a child, and he wouldn't start now. He ran his hands through his hair, his stomach tightening.

Leeroy was dead. His best friend had been *murdered*.

"They'll pay, Leeroy. Every last one of those fuckers will pay. I swear to *GOD* they will!"

James spun on his heel and marched to the basement

door. Unlike the simple locks on most of his doors, the steel-reinforced door to the basement was sealed with both tumbler- and key-based physical locks, in addition to a palm scanner. A thick coat of dust indicated the Harriken hadn't tried to enter the basement, arguably the only important area in his whole house. That made sense. They'd come to deliver a single bloody message. No other room had been disturbed.

Too bad. James liked the idea of some Harriken getting taken out by his traps. The door couldn't easily be kicked in, and if the locks weren't disabled, any intruder would have to be bulletproof and then some.

James grabbed his keys from his pocket and went to work. He threw his hand on the palm scanner.

The seething cauldron of rage stomped down into the basement where the tools of his trade were carefully stacked on labeled shelves or hanging on the walls: electronics, melee weapons, pistols, rifles, explosives, and magical items, among other things—almost everything a man might need when he was hunting down some heavily armed or magical target.

James hadn't bothered to restrict it to legal equipment, either. It was a one-stop shop for a man when he needed to get *complicated.* If he didn't have it here, he had it in the warehouse.

KISS.

That was what he *liked* to do, but the Harriken had apparently decided they wanted things complicated, even after he'd been forgiving enough not to snap their two enforcers in half. They'd picked a fight they hadn't needed to pick, so now it was time for KIBACS: keep it bloody and complicated, stupid.

James cracked his knuckles. "You shouldn't have fucked with my dog. I hope you enjoy your short-assed lives."

James crept into the church, residual reverence dulling his rage only a small amount. Guilt didn't gnaw at him for what he was about to do to the Harriken, but you always respected a man in his own house—and a church was God's house.

The nave was empty. Candles lined the area, casting their flickering light all around and producing sinister shadows. They seemed to James like portents of the bloody rage-storm about to be unleashed in the city.

James marched over to the confessional, slid open the door, and stepped inside. He took a few deep breaths. No priest would approve of what he was about to say, but that didn't mean he wouldn't say it.

"It's been a few days, child," said the familiar Jersey-accented voice of Father McCartney from the other side of the screen.

"Bless me father, for I'm *about* to sin," James rumbled. "A lot."

"Mankind is fallen. We are destined to sin. It is through our Lord's sacrifice that we find forgiveness and repentance." The priest let out a faint sigh. "So what is to be the nature of your transgression, child?"

James didn't hesitate. "Killing, and lots of it."

"But the Lord orders us to abide his commandments, including 'Thou shalt not kill.'"

"Depending on the translation, isn't it, 'Thou shalt not murder?'"

Father McCartney chucked. "A theologian now, are we, child? Okay, let me ask you this: do you intend to kill in self-defense?"

"No," James admitted. "I intend to kill them in vengeance."

"Then I think most would view what you plan as murder. Is there nothing I can say to dissuade you from the path of blood you're about to walk?"

"I know it's probably wrong, but that's why I'm here," the bounty hunter said. "But I also can't let this go, Father. They've taken too much. They've gone too far."

The memory of Leeroy's desecrated body flashed in James' mind. His hands curled into fists, and he sucked in a breath through his teeth.

"I see." The priest's seat creaked. "How many people do you intend to kill, then, to sate your vengeance?"

"All of them," James spat through gritted teeth. "Every...last...one."

"And how have these men wronged you, James, to bring such anger? What have they taken from you? Your job is important and you deal with darkness most of us will never know, but you don't normally let your temper run away with you. It's like my father used to tell me: don't let someone live rent-free in your head."

It wasn't lost on James that Father McCartney had switched to using his actual name and dropped the all-wise priest act. That was what the priest always did when he started seriously worrying about the bounty hunter's soul.

James dug his nails into his palms. "They killed Leeroy, Father."

The bounty hunter held no illusions about his soul. Heaven wouldn't take him, and Hell probably would be too scared to let him in.

"May the Lord have mercy," Father McCartney exclaimed.

"On them?" James bellowed, shaking with rage. "They don't *deserve* mercy."

"No, James. On you. I'm sorry for your loss, and I understand what that dog meant to you. I also understand why you feel you must kill these men, but I need to ask you something. Let's be straight now, James. Are these men innocents otherwise? Are you sure this wasn't an accident? You already walk a thin line. Make sure you're not about to cross it."

James took several deep breaths. He lived his life with carefully cultivated and controlled anger, but in this case a true burning rage had pushed past all his limits. It took a lot of effort for him not to punch the confessional's wall.

"Innocents? No. This was the Harriken. They butchered Leeroy and left him on a serving tray for me to find. They wanted me to know it was them. They think they are teaching me a lesson, so I'm going to return the fu—the favor."

Father McCartney fell silent for a good five seconds before answering, "Then I will pray for their poor lost souls, for they have violated the Eleventh Commandment: 'Thou shalt not kill a man's best friend.'" The priest let out a weary sign, obviously troubled by the death about to be dealt but having trouble working up the will to stop it. "I will pray for your soul as well, James. Do what you have to, but remember that this world still needs you. Be careful."

"Don't worry, Father," James replied, sliding the booth open. "The only person who won't die tonight is me."

Shay pulled her bright-red Fiat Spider to the curb at Brownstone's house. She wasn't even sure why she'd bothered to come. Maybe some part of her wanted to confirm that the man was gay so she could explain why he hadn't made any moves. Checking out his house would help her gather evidence.

On the other hand, if Brownstone *wasn't* gay, he might make a pass at her in a more comfortable setting. Then she would have the satisfaction of knowing she was right about all men, including James Brownstone.

It'd help for Shay to get to know the bounty hunter better anyway. She didn't have to, or even want to, be his friend, but it would help when working together on future jobs. The more in sync they were, the better the chance they'd both come out of it alive and richer.

Whatever the treasure hunter thought about James' personality, she acknowledged that he was a first-class fearless ass-kicker and a good guy to have on your side in a fight. Warlocks weren't normally so easily killed. If they were, the world be a lot safer.

Shay threw open her Fiat's door and stepped out. She walked to Brownstone's front door and knocked several times. No answer. She repeated the process with no greater success.

"Are you even here?" Shay grumbled. That was what she got for not bothering to call ahead. For all she knew Brownstone was out drinking with Smite-Williams, or getting laid.

A light breeze blew, and a metallic scent reached her nose.

Shay's heartrate increased, and she slid her gun out of her shoulder holster. It was always better to be overly cautious. She lacked the nose of a shifter, but she'd been around enough bloody messes to easily recognize even a faint whiff.

After a quick check of the nearby area, the treasure hunter splayed herself against the wall and made her way to the corner of the house. The breeze brought the smell, which suggested a source outside the house. The lack of an obvious body in the front told her the body she presumed she would find lay out back. She reached the corner and took a deep breath.

Gun raised, she whipped around the corner. No enemies or gunfire greeted her—only silence and an empty side yard.

Don't be dead, Brownstone. No man who can kill three warlocks like that should get taken out like a bitch at his own house.

Careful steps brought her into the backyard.

A small cardboard cross caught Shay's attention. It stood atop the disturbed soil of a freshly-dug grave, another sight she was distressingly familiar with.

Shay slipped her gun back into her holster and peered

down at the grave. The cardboard wouldn't last long, and the grave was too new. All signs pointed to a recent burial, if not that day.

"Leeroy" was the sole word on the cross.

The dog.

James had talked about him briefly during their time on the planes. It was one of the few times the guy had seemed normal to her; even pleasant. Another gust blew and the cardboard swayed in the wind, revealing more writing on the back.

"Remember," Shay read. Kanji characters had been printed next to the English word. "Oh, shit."

Shay didn't know Japanese, but she did know the Japanese characters for Harriken.

"It's got nothing to do with me," Shay muttered to herself. "It's not…" She sighed, her palm going to her forehead. "That's just low, Harriken. Too damn low."

Killing someone who had it coming was one thing. Hell, killing someone who didn't have it coming but could at least defend themselves was justifiable—depending on the circumstances—but killing some poor dog who didn't have a chance was over the line. The kind of men who did that had no limits.

The treasure hunter swallowed. She knew about people with no limits.

Shay knelt and found a large rock. She pulled out her knife and scratched Leeroy's name, the current year, and "You will be avenged" underneath. She wished she knew what year the dog had been born so she could add it to the stone. Maybe she'd ask Brownstone the next time she saw him, if he'd not gotten himself killed already.

"Damn it." Shay stood and walked back toward her Spider. Leeroy's death had nothing to do with her, but that didn't mean she was going to let Brownstone get himself killed. She had a pretty good idea where he would be partying that night.

A sick smirk grew on her face. The good thing about the Harriken being such arrogant douchebags was that they didn't hide much. They didn't think they had anything to fear. Anyone in Los Angeles with an ounce of street knowledge knew the location of their headquarters.

"Am I really going to do this?" Shay muttered to herself. She started the car. "Fuck it. I was bored anyway." She slammed down the accelerator and peeled out.

9

James parked his truck several blocks away from the old two-story white Victorian the Harriken used as their local headquarters. He snorted—something about the house didn't fit the band of murderous Japanese thugs. Maybe its aesthetic would fit them better once he painted over all that with their blood.

His gathered knowledge on the enemy amounted to exactly jack, with shit for actionable intel. He knew their typical enforcer strength and weapon choices, but he had no idea how many men might be inside the house or if they had access to heavier weapons or magic. Somehow that didn't bother him, though. If the Harriken were actually badasses, they would have proven it already.

So far his personal encounters with them had involved them picking on a girl and a dog, so these fuckers came off as glorified bullies. They needed to learn the most important lesson: there was *already* somebody bigger out there.

Hell, he knew it. He wouldn't be but a fucking snack to a large dragon.

James stepped onto the street and patted his holsters and pockets to confirm his loadout in the duster he'd swapped his leather jacket for. Multiple magazines, pistols, and knives: check. A frag grenade and a flashbang just in case: check.

It would be more than enough to clear out a house filled with sword- and pistol-wielding gangsters. The Harriken didn't represent the kind of threat that called for magic or heavy explosives, let alone his necklace.

Besides, a vengeance run required a personal touch. Blowing the entire house up from outside wouldn't be as satisfying as going through beating down or killing every single motherfucking dog-killing Harriken.

Despite what he'd told Father McCartney, James wasn't sure if he was going to kill everyone in the house. Someone needed to survive, if only so they could pass along to others what happened when you fucked with something or someone the Granite Ghost cared about.

James grabbed some binoculars from the seat and examined the house and its surroundings. Two guards stood upfront, armed with *wakizashis* and pistols. Like the Harriken he'd seen before, they wore dark suits, but hints of their extensive tattoos peeked out on their necks and hands. Several security drones surveilled the area around the headquarters.

He didn't care about the drones or the guards. They made his job easier. Stealth wasn't on the menu. The Harriken needed to know he was coming. If they were aware that he was coming, they would be afraid.

Their fear might help him in the battle, but that wasn't the point. Leeroy must have been plenty scared when they captured and killed him, and he would make the bastards feel the dog's pain and fear tenfold. The Harriken would wet themselves before James sent them to Hell. Maybe the Devil would chop them up and feed them to dog demons.

James cracked his knuckles and stuck his hands in his pocket, then strolled down the street humming *The Volga Boatman.* He wasn't sure why he chose that song. It just seemed like a good tune to kill a bunch of men to.

When he was a block out, the two guards frowned and glanced down at their watches before spinning his way. They probably had a feed from the security drones. Their hands dropped to their sword hilts, but they didn't go for their guns.

Big mistake. They might have had a ghost of a chance if they'd opened fire on him immediately. James continued his casual stroll from the sidewalk to the path leading through the well-manicured lawn to the front door. The guards fixed their glares on him, but they hadn't moved otherwise. The bounty hunter closed to a distance where they could have easily put a few rounds into him.

"Hey, assholes," James rumbled. "Just to be clear, this is Harriken headquarters, right? I'd hate to waste my time busting up the wrong place."

One of the guards spat. "You will leave now if you value your life, James Brownstone. You have already offended the Harriken. We would have thought our little message to you would have convinced you of the stupidity of opposing us, but now you come here and disrespect us *again.*"

"Yeah, about that...you really trying to tell me you're super-badass because you murdered an innocent dog?"

James inhaled and ran a hand over his bald head. "Because that strikes me as a pussy move, you stupid son of a bitch."

The douchebags might have received a modicum of mercy if they had shown some remorse. Instead, they were doing everything they could to antagonize him more.

The Harriken snorted and spat again, this time at the bounty hunter's feet. "You are one ugly piece of pork, Brownstone. I think you'll look better after we carve *you* up."

The two guards laughed and drew their swords.

Douchebag One pointed his sword at James. "You're as stupid as that whiny little bitch of a dog we killed."

The bounty hunter sighed. It was like the guys were begging him to kill them. Well, people should always get what they want, if not what they deserve.

James shot forward and slammed his fist into Douchebag One's head. The Harriken sailed backward, crashing so hard into the door that the wood cracked.

Douchebag Two slashed with his blade, but the bounty hunter jerked to the side. The sword met nothing but air.

The Harriken tried to bring his blade back, but it was too late; James grabbed his hand and squeezed until the bones cracked. The man let out a scream, which was silenced by the bounty hunter's elbow smashing his wind-pipe. He collapsed to the ground, gurgling and gasping for breath.

"The only ugly and stupid motherfuckers around here are you bastards."

James glanced at the first douchebag. The Harriken still breathed, but the blood running down his head and his closed eyes proved he wouldn't be getting up anytime soon.

It was his lucky day. He'd live to tell the epic story of how James Brownstone killed everyone else in the house.

"At least put up a fucking fight," James grumbled.

He reached for the door. Locked. A keypad sat next to the door. He didn't have time for this shit.

James snatched up the gurgling Harriken with both hands, holding him by his neck and hip.

"Huh, a good two hundred pounds, I'd say. Perfect. Time to get a little medieval on you guys."

He swung the man back and then slammed him straight into the door. After a sickening *crunch*, the wood splintered and the man stopped gurgling.

Frowning, James eyed the body and then flipped the Harriken so he was feet-first. Three more blows knocked the door off one of its hinges, and a loud alarm screeched inside.

"Now we're talking." James tossed the body to the ground, ripped the door the rest of the way off, and tossed it onto the front lawn.

A half-dozen Harriken enforcers stood inside the foyer with their swords drawn. Anger radiated from their faces.

Irritation flared in James. He didn't want them angry. He wanted them afraid.

"You assholes are going to have to up your game if you want to win," James yelled. "But if you get on your knees and beg Leeroy's forgiveness, maybe I'll kill you quickly. Otherwise, no guarantees."

"Who the fuck is Leeroy?" one of the men yelled.

He slumped to the ground a second later, one of James'

knives embedded in his throat. The surviving Harriken hissed and stepped back. The attack had come so fast they'd barely had time to register it before their friend lay dying in a pool of his own blood and arrogance.

The shrill alarm cut out, but no more reinforcements arrived. A dark laugh escaped the bounty hunter's mouth. The idiots thought they could hold him in the front.

James looked each man in the eye in turn. "Leeroy was the fucking dog you murdered, you sons of bitches!"

At least the Harriken were bright enough not to charge him one at a time. He'd give them credit for that. Three rushed him from the front, while two circled on opposite sides.

James didn't wait around to get stabbed. He unleashed two more throwing knives, nailing the would-be back-stabbers.

Each flanker collapsed with a moan and a knife embedded in their hearts. They weren't dead yet, but they soon would be.

James leapt back, dodging sword strikes from two of the men in front. A quick feint by the bounty hunter left the third man exposed, and James' foot was happy to take advantage of the opportunity. The Harriken sailed through the room until he smashed halfway through a wall.

The remaining two killers exchanged glances and swallowed.

"Good," James said. "Glad to see you're finally afraid. Keep in mind that I haven't even pulled a gun yet, fuckers."

He charged again, narrowly ducking a blade, and a rising uppercut sent his attacker into the ceiling. The Harriken's head bent nearly to a right angle and his neck snapped with a loud *crunch*, then the body fell to the ground with a *thud*. The collision decorated the ceiling with a dent. James had to admire the strength of the building materials in this home.

He wondered if it had ever been on HGTV? He'd seen a lot of interesting houses on various Home and Garden Television shows.

The other Harriken broke for the stairs. A pussy didn't deserve a respectful death. James whipped out his .45 and put three tightly-clustered rounds into the fucker's back. His victim screamed and collapsed, then rolled down the stairs. His sword clattered and fell through the slats of the bannister to the floor. It embedded itself tip-first.

"Someone come out here and try and pull the sword from the floor," James bellowed. "Maybe you'll become King of all Los Angeles."

Yelling and murmuring in English and Japanese reached his ears from both upstairs and from behind a reinforced door he spotted on the other side of the living room. He presumed it led to a basement, which was probably where the gangsters kept everything important. His gaze shifted between the stairs and the door.

The guys upstairs had nowhere to go, but there was a chance that the Harriken had escape tunnels downstairs. If he left his back open, he might end up flanked by the enemy on both sides. Part of being a badass was not being a *dumbass*.

Movement from above caught his attention. Several more Harriken rushed to the landing on the stairs, this time with pistols out instead of swords. His enemy had made the decision for him.

"Kill that *oni* fucker!" screamed one of the men.

James dove toward a connected dining room as bullets pelted the ground where he'd been seconds before. Soon they pierced the wall all around him.

He took a few deep breaths as his heart pounded. He didn't regret not going all-out when he'd equipped himself. Killing all the Harriken without every possible advantage was his way of showing contempt to the enemy who'd murdered his dog.

James readied his weapon and then darted sideways, exposing himself for only a second as he pulled the trigger of his .45 several times. Three Harriken fell to the ground, crimson stains blossoming on their chests. An enemy bullet grazed his chest, and he hissed at the pain.

Who gives a fuck? Leeroy had felt a lot more pain than this.

Loud shots echoed as the Harriken unloaded their magazines. Plaster and wood exploded from the wall, filling the room with dust and coating James. It mingled with the blood splatters already on him.

The gunfire stopped. James listened, but couldn't make out the murmuring. A familiar slap and metallic click sounded from upstairs.

Well, shit.

Someone had upgraded to something able to spew a lot more bullets. James rushed to the other side of the room as a hail of bullets destroyed what was left of his make-shift fortification.

His quick dodge not only saved his life, but gave him the location of a Harriken shooting an AK. James didn't pause for a second, instead pivoting and rushing toward the opening. The Harriken perforated the wall, realizing too late that their target had decided on full offense.

A bullet between the eyes brought down Captain AK. James didn't even try to dodge as he gunned down the rest of the shooters. Dead bodies littered the stairs and the ground now. Pools of blood were starting to merge into lakes.

Not done yet. Not done at all.

James ejected his empty magazine and slipped in a new one. Fire blossomed in his shoulder with the movement. He'd taken a round to the shoulder. He snorted in derision.

The bodies now littering the stairs were probably the men who'd been on the second floor, but James couldn't take any chances. After retrieving his knives he bounded up the stairs, dodging through the bodies like some sort of twisted obstacle course.

Several doors lay open. A quick sweep revealed only beds and a room with a huge TV and couches. Comfy.

One door at the end of a hallway remained closed. James raised his gun and emptied his entire magazine into the door. He swapped mags and crept toward the door, looking for shadows blocking the holes.

Movement caught his eye, and James sprinted forward. A powerful kick sent the door sailing off his hinges and a screaming Harriken charged him, not with a *wakizashi* but with a *katana*.

This fool must have been higher-ranking, since he wasn't in a suit but a man's red kimono. His hair was up in a topknot, and anger blazed in his eyes.

Again, not what James wanted.

James snapped his .45 up, blocking the blade, and the

clang of metal on metal rang through the hall. The man recovered far quicker than any of the guards had, slashing at his opponent again in the blink of an eye.

A quick dodge saved James' neck. He tried to squeeze off a round, but the gun jammed. Red Samurai gave a feral grin, thinking he had the upper hand.

With a scream, he charged at James and swung his blade. James pivoted to the Harriken's side as he grabbed his K-Bar in one fluid movement. Red Samurai tried to match his movement, only to get a knife jammed into his throat for his trouble.

James let go of the knife and the man slumped to the ground, his eyes wide.

The bounty hunter sneered at the dying man. "'Don't take a knife to a gunfight.' They don't say shit about taking one to a swordfight."

James picked up the jammed .45 and stuck it in a holster. He had another couple of pistols if he needed them. After yanking the K-Bar out of the man's throat, he cleaned it on the guy's kimono.

Two levels clear. One basement to go.

10

Shay's initial plan had been to do a quick recon of the house; just a simple drive-by to check out the number of guards out front. That plan ended the second she spotted the two downed Harriken guards near the front of the house. The broken and cracked front door lying on the lawn made it clear that Brownstone had already begun his revenge assault.

"Subtle," Shay muttered.

Still, she could admire the direct approach. Killing someone should be an up-close and personal affair. If you didn't get a little blood on you, you were being a pussy.

Of course, charging in the front door was its own special form of moronic. A smarter play would have been to go around the back or climb up the side for a second-story entry. Strolling in the entrance went past moronic to downright insane.

At least for most men. Brownstone had proven once again that he wasn't like most men. Not even close.

During the entire drive over, Shay had kept trying to

tell herself that it wasn't her business. It had nothing to do with field archaeology. Nothing to do with her.

Still, somehow she'd convinced herself to drive halfway across town to attack Harriken headquarters and help avenge the murder of the dog of a guy she didn't even like that much.

Plus, the fucker didn't even seem to find her hot.

You better damn well be gay, Brownstone.

Frustrating didn't even begin to describe the situation. Idiotically frustrating, maybe.

"What the hell am I doing?" Shay ran her hands through her dark hair and sighed.

Brownstone was already inside, and the angry fool might need her help. If she didn't help him out, the next person who ended up in a shallow grave might be her. The Harriken might go after all the bounty hunter's associates.

The assholes had murdered a dog. It wasn't like she could be assured that there was no photo of her standing beside her recent partner. The Harriken were thorough when they felt they had been disrespected.

Self-preservation served as a nice excuse for Shay to help. It was time to get involved.

Shay parked along the street and rolled her window down. She waited for thirty seconds, listening for the sounds of closing sirens. She didn't want to tangle with a deploying SWAT team. Shooting at criminal scum was one thing, pissing off the authorities quite another.

The last thing she needed was for anyone to go digging into her past. She'd worked too hard to escape it.

Not even a hint of approaching cops reached her ears. Even the nearest cars sounded far away.

It was just a nice, quiet little neighborhood street where a man was engaged in the bloody revenge-fueled massacre of a ruthless criminal gang.

If that didn't scream *AMERICA!*, nothing did.

The neighbors probably knew not to get involved in Harriken business, and the cops might have been paid to look the other way. In either event, the circumstances granted her what she needed most: time to check things out.

Taking a look inside didn't mean she was committing to dying to pull Brownstone out of his own shit.

After a quick pat of her holster and sheath, Shay threw the car door open and stepped outside.

"I'm as stupid as Brownstone," she muttered to herself, drawing her gun. "Not even gonna make any money off this shit."

Shay rushed toward the house in a zigzag pattern. Assuming the entire enemy force had been completely devastated might get her killed. For all she knew, Brownstone was bleeding out inside, and a Harriken sniper was aiming down his sights and waiting for reinforcements to pick off. Helpful reinforcements like her.

The frustrated field archaeologist's arrival at the front door remained uncontested. No sniper blew her head off.

Nice night so far.

The front door more closely resembled a front *hole*. Two Harriken enforcers lay on the ground. One man's head hung at an unnatural angle, and his head and face were smashed in from what looked like extreme blunt-force trauma.

Shay eyed the body with clinical detachment,

wondering if Brownstone's punches could do that kind of damage. Whether or not they could, the even and wide bruising patterns didn't support that theory. Something else had killed the man.

What kind of weapon did you use, Brownstone? Did you show up with a shovel or something?

Killing the men with the shovel he had used to bury his dog would be poetic. And badass.

Her gaze traveled to the hole and then to the cracked and bloodstained door lying on the lawn. Her eyes widened.

No, not a shovel.

"What the fuck?" Shay whispered.

Did you seriously use a guy as a battering ram, Brownstone? I don't know if I'm impressed or fucking terrified. Guess a little of both.

The other bloodied man's face remained intact, which was probably why he could still let out a quiet moan. The tomb raider jerked her gun toward the man, but quickly realized he wasn't a threat. His mangled buddy would need a closed-casket funeral.

Shay squatted next to the guy and considered her options. Taking him out would be easy enough, but she sensed that Brownstone wanted the guy alive for some reason. There was no way the bounty hunter wouldn't have finished the Harriken off otherwise. Brownstone had broken down a door using a man's body. Restraint in the application of violence didn't seem to be one of his virtues.

Gonna interrogate this bastard later, Brownstone? Is that the idea? Should have pinned a note on his back so I didn't waste my time.

The Harriken moaned again.

"It's either your lucky day," Shay began, "or the worst fucking day of your life. Guess you'll find out later." She kicked him hard in the head to knock him out again.

A charnel house awaited Shay inside. Bodies littered the crimson-soaked floor and stairs and blood dripped a slow and steady beat to the floor from some of the corpses on the stairs, a metronome of carnage. One poor fucker was half-embedded in the wall like some bizarre wall decoration.

Salvador Dali meets Ed Gein.

"Jesus, Brownstone. How did you even get him through there?" she wondered aloud.

No pity pricked her heart for the dead Harriken. They'd pissed off the wrong man, and now they were paying the price. Any halfway decent criminal organization knew who to poke and who to leave alone. She hoped whoever was responsible for Harriken intelligence was lying in this room or on the stairs.

Organized crime was like any other business. Cost and benefit needed to balance, and the executive committee meeting on this fuckup was something she would pay big money to listen to.

Shay swept the room and a few other connected rooms, her gun ready, but spotted no active enemies. She headed back into the front room. The walls on the opposite side were perforated with dozens of jagged holes, some small, some large.

It's a goddamn warzone.

The treasure hunter took a few steps forward, looking down at the bodies on the floor. She didn't lower her gun.

One surprise Harriken ambush and she could end up dead.

Shay furrowed her brow and thought about every piece of evidence she'd seen so far.

Let's see... No shell casings outside. The guards' guns hadn't even been drawn, which meant they hadn't shot. Brownstone must have walked right up, and they had probably talked some shit back and forth. Didn't use anything but his hands, most likely.

The big guy entered through the front after bashing it open with a Harriken *guy's body. Killed these guys on the floor. No gun, all knives and fists.* Damn *could that guy hit hard. What the hell was he?*

Shay blinked and looked up at the large dent in the ceiling.

Seriously, Brownstone? How did you hit a guy all the way up there?

The fight in Peru had taken place in too small a space and over too short a time span for her to witness Brownstone's true strength. She exhaled slowly, glad that the guy seemed calm most of the time. She could only imagine what would happen if he decided to go from being merely an asshole to a murderous asshole.

Shay's focus shifted back and forth between the bodies and the bullet-riddled walls. Brownstone had obviously used the walls for cover. She doubted the shooters had engaged him until after the first wave of men had died at his hands.

That made sense. The Harriken must have banked on the men on the first floor outnumbering their enemy, but sometimes quantity *didn't* have a quality all its own.

Shay didn't spot any throwing knives in the stair bodies. Large holes marked the bodies, mostly around the chest. She walked to the bottom of the stairs and rolled one of the bodies over. Smaller entry wound in the front, bigger exit wound in the back—she'd seen that before.

So Brownstone took cover behind the swiss cheese walls of death there and started taking these guys out...with what? Probably a large-caliber pistol with hollow-points. So this wasn't just defense; he wanted to make sure he took the guys down. Definitely not trying to take a lot of prisoners. Also meant that Brownstone didn't think he was going to have to shoot through a lot of walls.

Shay chewed on that thought for a few seconds. Brownstone had assaulted the headquarters, motivated by vengeance. He might have wanted to see his enemies die in front of him.

Not unexpected.

She padded toward the dining room, keeping her gun ready. No bloodstains or bodies presented themselves on the floor, but .45-caliber brass shell casings lay all over. She performed a quick count.

Had to change mags at least once in here, I'm guessing. Probably only once, though.

A small amount of blood stained a side wall. Shay looked between the hole-pocked walls and the wall with blood, aiming her gun to help her visualize the line of fire.

Brownstone took a hit. Not enough to take him down, obviously.

Closer inspection of the wall led Shay to spot a small bullet hole.

So he took a hit, but the bullet passed clean through. Good for him, and lucky the Harriken *weren't using hollow-points too.*

Shay shook her head as she headed back toward the stairs. Violence was an art in and of itself, and the gory scene at the house proved that Brownstone was the fucking Jackson Pollock of ass-kicking.

A few quiet moans sounded from the stairs. Shay rushed into the front room, hurrying behind a couch, gun drawn. A sprint to a chair followed. No Harriken popped up to shoot at her, so she approached the source of the moans: two survivors.

Sloppy, Brownstone. Then again, these guys are obviously gonna bleed out.

"Help...me," one of the men groaned. "Can...pay...you. Earn...respect of the...Harriken."

"Yeah, about that... First, I just got a big paycheck today, so I'm not as impressed with money. Second, it doesn't make much sense to help out the guys who got their asses kicked and piss off the guy who did the ass-kicking. Sorry."

Shay tossed her pistol into her other hand and yanked out her knife, then walked to the man, pulled his head up, and slit his throat. The other moaner met his end right after. A quick check of the other bodies confirmed no more survivors, but she sliced their throats to be certain.

Stray thoughts about the Rod of Supay filtered into her head, and Shay resisted the urge to head-shoot all the corpses. Not only would it waste ammo, but she wasn't even sure that worked on zombies in real life.

Keeping her gun ready, the woman crept up the stairs and along the wall—more like a member of the SAS than a field archaeologist. She swept into each room, ready to shoot at any target presenting himself.

Each upstairs room stood empty, except for one containing a dead man with a katana beside him and a huge puncture wound in his throat. Shay stared at a bullet-riddled door lying against the wall opposite the open doorway.

Okay. Brownstone thought someone might be hiding, so he opened up on the door—or maybe he just was trying to see something. Why the knife? Downstairs showed that he's got good aim. Not a single sloppy shot in the bunch, and he was under fire probably the whole time.

Shay furrowed her brow as she tried to piece the clues together.

Katana guy must have gotten the drop on him, otherwise Brownstone would have put a bullet into his head or chest. Or three bullets.

From the look of things, this guy was high-ranking. Harriken do place a lot of importance in personal ass-kicking ability. Maybe Topknot Boy knocked Brownstone's gun out of his hand?

She spoke to the corpse. "You probably thought you had him, didn't you?" Shay snickered.

She crept out of the room, pointing her gun downward as she approached the stairs. There was only one major area left to explore, and that lay behind the reinforced door to what she assumed was the basement. After a trip through the killing fields, she closed on the door.

Someone, presumably Brownstone had fired a shitload of bullets into the door to create a hole where the lock used to be. A huge pile of shell casings lay near the door, and she knelt to inspect them.

Only a few were .45s. Most were 5.45×39mm.

James opened up with what...probably an AK? Did you run in here with two guns, Brownstone, like some VR shooter sim?

No. That's not right. The fuckers on the stairs all looked like they died from pistol wounds. Probably some Harriken *guy showed up with the AK, and Brownstone took him out and then took his gun to use as the world's bluntest lockpick.*

Shay searched around and found the expected rifle, snapped into two pieces shoved under one of the bodies. Brownstone was covering his back.

A full picture of the assault crystalized in her mind. Brownstone hadn't approached the headquarters with anything resembling stealth. Had never planned to. He'd boldly walked right up, knocked a guy out, and beat his partner to death in the process of using the man as a living battering ram.

Well, semi-living.

Outnumbered and outgunned, the bounty hunter had executed all his enemies while taking only a hit or two.

All because these men had killed his dog.

James Brownstone was a living bulldozer crossed with a tank designed in Hell.

Shay shook her head as she processed it all. The fight against the warlocks hadn't demonstrated one-tenth of this lethality. Anyone picking a fight with Brownstone should schedule their funeral ahead of time to save their relatives the trouble.

A couple of *thuds* sounded from downstairs, and Shay

nodded to herself. Brownstone didn't need her assistance. The death tableau had proved that.

I can still walk away. The Emperor of Destruction here doesn't need my help. Leeroy has been avenged, and then some.

Shay stared at the basement door and shook her head. "This is stupid." She sighed and grabbed the handle.

James gritted his teeth and flexed his arm. His shoulder ached from the bullet wound, and a burning sensation radiated from his side. Not the worst pain he'd ever been in, but not exactly fun either.

He stared down at the two dead Harriken at his feet with bullet holes between their eyes. They'd probably been the most impressive all night, given that they'd managed to slice his side with their swords.

The man who shot him would receive no respect. Throw enough lead in the air and you were bound to hit something. If they'd been fighting one-on-one James might have given him a little mental fist-bump.

The glint of gold caught James' attention.

The bounty hunter knelt and pulled a gold watch off one of the dead men. The cops didn't pay as much money for dead bounties, and the dead gangster wasn't going to need it anymore.

The fucker had probably bought it with drug and sex-slavery money anyway.

James pulled a silver ring off the other man and stood. Once he finished the last few Harriken, he'd have to take a few minutes to collect the smaller valuables. Not exactly evil blood warlock-level money, but at least it was something. He could cover the cost of ammo, if nothing else.

He took several breaths, doing his best to ignore the aches in his shoulder and side. Only one damned room remained in the basement.

Two low voices exchanged some curt words in Japanese behind the door. That didn't mean there were only two men, but he hadn't encountered more than two or three in any of the previous rooms or the hallway.

The entire basement was divided into six small sealed cement-and-metal rooms linked by a central cement hallway lit by fluorescent lights. A nice, oppressive vibe—all very East Germany circa 1980. He wondered why the assholes didn't invest in some LEDs, already.

Most of the small rooms were nothing more than store-rooms for weapons and drugs. One room appeared to be an in-house tattoo parlor. Another was the security center for the house, with live feeds from the drones.

James wasn't the Professor, but as far as he could tell none of the rooms contained magical artifacts. Though he couldn't confirm that, it wasn't like he could haul the entire contents of the Harriken house back to his place.

The cops would show up eventually, and even if they did like James, he didn't want to spend a lot of time answering questions. Plus, there was the small matter of the dozens of homicides he'd just committed.

Unfortunately "he needed killing" wasn't a valid legal defense in the state of California, no matter what Father McCartney had said about the Eleventh Commandment.

Going through each room and methodically killing every remaining Harriken had grown tedious, but at least James had ensured that almost everyone in the building that night now lay dead or close to death. From what he could tell, the remaining men had hoped they could wear him down or surprise him. Kicking in wooden doors and then shooting them made the last floor almost trivial compared to the massed attacks upstairs—except for the lucky side slashers.

Should have grabbed more watches.

James furrowed his brow and ran to the first storeroom. His first inspection only found boxes filled with drugs. He shoved those aside.

After popping a few more lids off boxes, James discovered one containing diamonds and another containing several gold necklaces.

"Jackpot! Sweetheart, I'll be back for you in a second," he murmured.

James stepped out of the room and marched toward the end of the hallway. It was time to clear the final room. He pulled the magazine out of his pistol...only to find he didn't have another one. Rather than switch to a back-up pistol, he holstered the weapon. Even though his arm and side hurt, the remaining few Harriken didn't worry him. With his bloodlust sated, his focus had fully returned. He wanted these last men to understand the depth of their mistake.

"If you surrender," he yelled. "I'll kill you quickly and

mercifully. Not planning to torture you or anything—not really my style—but I can't guarantee you won't suffer more if you fight me."

The last door flew open and two Harriken stepped out, swords in hand. James had to give it to these guys; at least they wouldn't die like little bitches. They stood no chance, so they were morons, but at least they were brave morons.

James flexed his arm, trying to fight the stiffness from the wound. "Congratulations, assholes."

The men narrowed their eyes. The one on the left gestured with his sword. "What are you playing at, *oni?*"

James barked out a low laugh and gestured to the trail of bodies and blood behind him. "Does this look like a fucking game to you, fuckhead? Anyway, congratulations. You're the last men standing, so you'll be the last to die. I don't know, maybe take some pride in that shit?"

"You're insane," said the man on the left, glancing behind James. "Totally insane."

The man on the right said nothing. His eyes screamed sweet fear.

At last *somebody* understood what Leeroy had gone through.

"*I'm* insane?" James took a single step forward. "Okay, before I kill your ass, explain that one to me."

"You do all this for a fucking animal?" Lefty argued. "A dog? You'd kill so many men over a pet? *No* animal is worth so many lives."

Neither anger nor fear burned in the man's eyes. Confusion reigned. James would kill him last. At least Righty finally understood the error of his ways.

James shrugged, the motion sending a spike of pain

through his shoulder. "You see, that's some bullshit. A dog doesn't matter?" He took another step forward. "Obviously Leeroy fucking mattered, or you douchebags wouldn't have butchered him and put him in my dining room." He pointed to Lefty. "So don't bitch to me now about dogs being less important than people, asshole. You and your people wanted to make a point, and you did. Now it's my turn, and I'm making *my* goddamn point."

The Harriken gripped his hilt so tightly his knuckles turned white. "Even if you kill us all here, we will be avenged. The Harriken will grow again, and wreak their vengeance on you and all you love."

James lifted an eyebrow. "That didn't work out so well for you last time, did it?" He shook his head. "All I had was a dog, and now all I have left is me."

Lefty's partner moved to the side. The attack would come soon.

James held up a hand and turned it back and forth, examining all the blood splatters. A little intimidation never hurt in a fight, although he wasn't sure how much of the blood was his and how much of it was from his enemies. It'd been a long time since he'd been forced to kill this many people at once.

"I already chose the douchebag at the entrance to be the lone survivor," James told them. "So what I'm guessing is that he goes and tells everyone how James Brownstone came in—by my-fucking-self, by the way—and took out an entire house filled with Harriken enforcers." He shook his head. "I think every fucking pussy left who remotely gives a shit about anyone in the house will pack up and run away. You fuckers thought you ruled through strength and fear." His eyes narrowed and his deep voice rumbled. "You don't know what strength and fear *are*."

Lefty and Righty charged, but James dodged by sprinting right past them. The surprised Lefty's sword missed his neck by under an inch.

James kicked the Harriken in the chest, sending him flying into a concrete wall. A dull *thud* echoed in the hallway and his sword clattered against the cement floor. He groaned, his eyes rolled up in his head, and he slumped.

Righty stabbed and swung with wild abandon. James dodged the attacks with ease, despite the flare of pain that came with every quick movement.

"You eat barbecue?" James asked conversationally as he ducked a stab.

The Harriken blinked and sliced at him, but this attack was no more successful than his previous ones.

"I said, 'Do you eat barbecue,' asshole?" James spoke a bit louder.

His opponent took a step back. Sweat beaded his brow, and his gaze kept darting to the side. He probably wanted to make a run for it, but James didn't care. The asshole wasn't escaping.

"What the fuck are you talking about, *oni?*"

"Barbecue. American-style, you know—not like *yakiniku*." James shrugged. "Nothing against it, just, I mean, gotta love the flavors of your homeland, right?"

The man blinked and shook his head as if he couldn't believe what he was hearing.

"That makes me think, though. You know, all these sauce flavors and different techniques—they're the result of different cultures in America blending together. English,

African, French, German, Mexican, on and on. It's some pretty deep shit if you actually get to studying the history."

The Harriken tried another few stabs, but James dodged them with even less effort. His attacker's face screamed panic now.

"Why are you talking about food?"

James gave the other man a demonic grin. "Food defines a culture. Fuck, food defines a culture in a way that a lot of things don't. I mean, shit, language? Plenty of people speak the same language, but don't eat the same shit. I was just thinking about whether I'm wrong to not want Oriceran ingredients in my sauces."

Lefty moaned and stirred on the floor. It was time to stop playing and finish things.

Righty's breathing grew ragged. *"Oni. Bakemono. Yokai.* I don't know what race you are, but *you're a monster."*

James shrugged, then winced at the pain. "Yeah, well, fuck you too." He sprinted forward, dodged the incoming attack and smashed his fist into the other man's face. The Harriken flew backward, smacking into the floor and rolling a good distance.

Groaning, the man tried to right himself, but James was already on him. The bounty hunter brought down his boot on the man's sword hand, crushing it. As the man screamed, James snatched up the *wakizashi* and sliced his head off with one clean stroke.

The bounty hunter turned toward Lefty. The remaining Harriken pulled himself to his feet and dropped his sword. His trembling hand pulled his pistol out of his holster.

The criminal let out a bitter laugh. "You're just fucking with us. I see. I understand."

James stalked toward the man, keeping his gaze on the pistol. He wasn't fast enough to dodge a bullet, but that wasn't the trick. The real skill came in predicting where an opponent might fire.

"Please enlighten me, asshole."

"This isn't about your dog."

James glowered at the other man. "Oh, this *is* about my fucking dog. If you would have left Leeroy alone, you'd all be breathing tomorrow instead of decomposing."

A shot rang out, but James had moved to the side before the man had even pulled the trigger. Another quick jerk put him out of the line of the fire for the next shot. By the third, he'd closed on Lefty and yanked his arm up. All the Harriken managed after that were several shots into the ceiling.

The bounty hunter's fist slammed into the man's stomach and Lefty doubled over in pain, gagging. He collapsed to the ground, clutching his stomach.

"Now," James growled, "you're gonna apologize to Leeroy on behalf of the Harriken."

S hay crept down the stairs, only to run into more of the aftermath of Hurricane Brownstone. The bottom of the stairwell led to a short corridor that turned to the right before joining a larger hallway. With the cement walls and stairwell, Brownstone would have been fed straight into a kill box.

Except he wasn't the one who was dead.

A dead Harriken lay against the wall, his face bruised, his eyes closed, and his nose askew. His sword had been driven right through his chest. Another man lay on the floor facedown, a pistol a few feet from his hand. His sword remained in its sheath.

Several flattened bullets littered the floor. Huge chips in the cement walls suggested the man had fired his pistol and missed his target.

Shay began to wonder how these final men could have believed they'd even have a chance against Brownstone. From what she could tell, they'd had fortifications and surprise...but still lost.

Maybe a few rocket launchers or some sort of powerful magic would have helped.

Brownstone's voice echoed from the other end of the basement, and the tomb raider sidled closer to him. She holstered her gun and peeked around the corner just in time to see the bounty hunter decapitate one man and rant about barbecue to the second before punching him in the stomach.

The only surprising thing about the sight was that Brownstone's second target didn't cough up blood and fall to the ground dead.

His survival told Shay that James must have pulled his punch. After everything she'd seen in Peru and in the house that night, she didn't believe a normal human could survive such a blow. She wasn't sure what Brownstone was —other than gay—but she refused to believe that he wasn't relying on some sort of magic. Normal people just weren't that strong.

James kicked the pistol behind the last man.

"I...apologize to the dog," the Harriken wheezed. "Please spare me."

"He wasn't just 'the dog.' He had a name." Brownstone crossed his arms and glared down at the man. "His fucking name was Leeroy."

"Okay, okay." The Harriken lifted his hand placatingly. "His name was Leeroy."

"You don't get it. I want you to apologize to Leeroy using his name."

"But he's dead."

"And you're gonna join him soon."

The gangster managed to sit up, though one hand still

rested on his stomach. A grimace seemed surgically attached to his face at this point. "But...you're really here because you want to know where she is, right?"

Brownstone crouched by the man. "I told you why I'm here. Because the Harriken murdered my dog."

"I told them not to do it. I told them we should leave you alone. I'd heard of you before."

"That's an interesting story, but even if I believed it, I don't fucking care." Brownstone scratched at an eyebrow. "You were telling me how the Harriken would grow stronger, get their vengeance on me and come after everyone I love. Don't you remember that?" He shrugged. "It wasn't exactly ages ago. I know I hit you pretty hard, so maybe your memory is a little fuzzy. And I seem to remember a speech implying my dog wasn't that important." He stood again. "Makes me question your honesty, fuckface."

The spectacle transfixed Shay. Whether Brownstone was offering a casual discussion of barbecue or threatening to kill the Harriken over his dog, the feral menace never left his deep, growling voice. The man's appetite for vengeance hadn't been sated, despite killing almost everyone else in the house. The purity of the brutality was as fascinating as it was unsettling. To call him a killing machine would be insufficient.

A force of nature, maybe.

"I apologize to Leeroy," the Harriken man said, now able to get his words out more steadily. "It was stupid of us to do what we did."

Brownstone snorted. "Stupid?"

The Harriken prostrated himself. "It was wrong. We

disrespected you. We disrespected Leeroy." The man kept his forehead pressed against the floor. "But we know you want her, too. We know that's why you've interfered with us."

Shay furrowed her brow. Brownstone hadn't mentioned much about his previous work during their job together, though now that she thought about it, it made sense that the Harriken must have had some decent reason to come after him.

Her first thoughts went to possible Harriken bounties, but the groveling gangster's words suggested something more complicated. She doubted Brownstone was involved in any sort of Harriken scheme. The bounty hunter didn't strike her as the type who would play too many sides against each other.

Shay didn't doubt his intelligence. It was more that she doubted his patience.

"Interfered with you?" Brownstone repeated. "It's more like when I go somewhere, you assholes show up and cause trouble for me." He let out a weary sigh. "And that first time, I was just trying to pay a favor back for someone who helped me find my dog. You see how that works? You help me with my dog, I help you. You kill my dog, I kill you. Fucking simple, right?"

The man on the ground swallowed, but didn't respond.

"Your first two guys could have turned around and left. Or you guys could have never come to my house. Or killed my dog." Brownstone shrugged. "If you'd refrained from doing that I wouldn't have gotten in your face. I wouldn't have had to kill any of you, just like I didn't kill those first two assholes. Fuck, I don't give a shit about bounties on small fry like you. It's not worth my time. Right now, I'm just trying to decide if I need two guys running around telling people why they shouldn't go after me, or only one. 'Cause I got one guy already upstairs still alive."

Shay nodded to herself. She'd been wrong about why Brownstone wanted the man alive, but she'd been smart not to kill him.

The gangster raised his head, his mouth pressed into a thin line. It was a hard thing to stare death right in the face. The man was used to being on the other end of this kind of exchange.

Some might call it karma in action.

Shay wondered if Brownstone really cared that much about bounty money. His skills meant he could have easily made a lot of cash if he were willing to help the right kind of corrupt people. An enforcer who could tear apart a house filled with armed men would be a useful weapon for plenty of organized crime groups, let alone terrorist groups, rogue nations, and God knew what sort of weirdos from Oriceran. In the chaos of the current world, it was smart to collect all the weapons you could.

Killing some blood-magic warlocks in a narrow tunnel was one thing, but the assault on the Harriken headquarters proved that Brownstone wasn't remotely allergic to violence, and didn't need self-defense as an excuse to kill.

Money couldn't be a big motivation for him, but then... The pieces didn't fit together, and Shay felt like she was missing something.

The tomb raider resisted a sigh. She didn't want to alert Brownstone to her presence.

She'd seen enough. The bounty hunter obviously didn't

need her help, and he could finish up with the remaining Harriken man without her spying on him. She stepped around the corner and crept back up the stairs, the sound of the conversation fading into the distance.

James stood in silence for a good minute, glaring down at the Harriken and trying to decide if he would kill the man or let him live. Not out of mercy, of course, but so that the gangster could tell anyone who'd listen what happened when people fucked with James Brownstone or anything he loved.

That was only part of his motivation for falling quiet. James had been so focused on watching the man that he almost missed it, but at last moment, he'd heard the faint footfalls of someone creeping down the stairs. Whoever it was probably hid down the hallway and listened to the exchange before they snuck back upstairs.

James had been waiting for them to come around the corner the entire time.

He chuckled. Some stupid Harriken, probably some idiot out buying cigarettes, had come back to the house and then chickened out after seeing the James' redecoration. The distraction's departure meant James was back to trying to decide the fate of the man kneeling in front of him.

"I'm honestly stumped whether I should kill you," he admitted.

"I-I didn't want to be involved with it," the Harriken man said. "I'll tell you where she is. You can get her then.

Sell her. Right? Let me live, and I'll tell you where. A man like you will know what to do with her."

James didn't have the remotest clue who the Harriken man was babbling about, but more to the point, he didn't care.

"Are you seriously trying to fucking negotiate with me? You don't get it, do you, asshole? Get it through your fucking head, already—you don't have anything I want, other than your life."

The other man wiped some sweat from his brow and trembled. "Mount Baldy. There's an old resort that's been converted to a private chalet. The Belmont House. She's there."

James scrubbed his face with a hand. "If it's not a bounty or not personal, I don't give a shit. And some Harriken shit on Mount Baldy is neither of those."

It was one thing to kill a man in battle, but he was having a hard time working up his bloodlust with this pathetic fool begging for his life and about to wet himself. Most of the house had been cleared.

Maybe that was enough.

The bounty hunter threw up a hand and turned to head down the hallway. "Guess it's your lucky day. You annoyed me into not killing you, and I think I made my point. Tell everyone you know what happened here and why. Make it fucking super-clear that if anyone even so much as sniffs around me without my permission, I will end them."

Even though the feeds from the security drones were likely being transmitted to a backup location, it wouldn't be good enough to just see him. Leaving survivors was still useful. He needed to be sure that everyone knew who had taken out the base, and the exact reasons why.

"I will," the man called from behind him.

James had made it halfway down the hall when he heard the scrape of metal on cement.

Fucker. I gave you more than enough chances.

He spun, his hand dropping to one of his backup pistols.

The Harriken man held his pistol, but hadn't stood yet. Maybe if he'd fired from a crouch, he would have had a chance.

Three quick 9mm bullets exploded from the bounty hunter's gun. The Harriken jerked with each shot before collapsing to the ground, groaning quietly. Blood leaked from his chest and mouth.

James holstered his weapon and stared at the man for a few seconds. He'd given the bastard more than a few chances, and even demonstrated a little forgiveness and mercy.

Father McCartney would be proud. He'd practically turned the other cheek. Well, only after killing a shit-ton of men, perhaps, but he had at least *tried*. Maybe he could count that as turning half a cheek. After all, he'd sworn to kill every last one of them and he hadn't, right? Did two wrongs make a right?

His shoulder and sides still burned. His coat might have been filled with the implements of death, but none of their opposites—not even a bandage. He kept more than a few first aid supplies in his truck, because he assumed that if he couldn't make it back to his truck he was probably dead.

The bounty hunter stopped at the bottom of the stairs.

Wait. I feel like I'm forgetting something.

James grunted. He'd almost forgotten the diamonds and jewelry.

He would have liked more time to liberate some valuables from the men he'd defeated, but he knew that since the shooting had stopped, somebody would be on their way to investigate. There was only so long a neighbor would tolerate dead guys in front of the house across the street.

Guess it's time to grab and dash.

13

S hay leaned against her Spider with her arms crossed. She'd thought about leaving, but wanted Brownstone to know she'd at least bothered to show up. Even if she didn't play well with others—especially men—that didn't mean the tomb raider didn't understand the importance of building trust.

Brownstone emerged from the house and glanced down at the Harriken Shay had knocked out earlier before looking at her. She gave him a quick, casual wave and waited for him to walk over to her.

"You're about the last person I expected to see here," Brownstone told her when he reached her. Weariness infused his voice, not unexpected after annihilating an entire house full of hardened killers.

Shay shrugged. "I wanted to talk to you, so I stopped by your house."

"And?"

"I got suspicious and poked around. I thought something had happened to you, and then I found Leeroy's grave. I'm sorry, Brownstone. You got dealt a shit hand."

"And why did you come here?" he asked, blunt as usual.

"You're a useful guy to have on treasure hunts. If you're gonna die, I'd prefer it be fighting off warlocks trying to steal zombie rods rather than random gangsters."

James grunted. "The only people who died tonight were Harriken."

Shay waved a hand dismissively. "Fair enough. Point is, I showed up and saw that everyone was dead inside. I figured you had it handled, and I didn't want to poke around in some spooky basement."

"You'll go into an Inca tomb, but a basement bothers you?" he wondered.

"Funny how that works." The tomb raider grinned.

Lying came easily and naturally to Shay, but a twinge of guilt hit her. She wasn't sure why she didn't want Brownstone to know she'd witnessed his encounter.

The bounty hunter grunted and nodded at the house. "I killed everyone in there except one guy at the door, as you know. I was going to let one more guy go, but he tried to take a shot at me."

"That was dumb."

"Yeah."

Shay stared into his eyes for a moment, looking for any sign of remorse. Failing to find that, she sought pleasure. She didn't find that either.

Brownstone had done what he needed to do to avenge his dog. Nothing more, nothing less.

Blood soaked his shirt on the side and on his shoulder.

The man's t-shirt was more a shredded rag than a piece of clothing at this point.

Shay had spotted the stiffness in his movements when she was watching him in the basement. This close to him, the bullet wound was obvious.

"Do I need to take you to the hospital?" She shrugged. "Or do you use some back-alley surgeon?"

Brownstone shook his head and gingerly moved his arm. "Bullet went clean through. I have a first-aid kit in my truck. I can just sew it up."

Shay eyed him with open disbelief. "You're tough, but you're not gonna be able to sew up your own shoulder with one hand." She sighed. "Fortunately for you, I've done this sort of thing before."

"Knew a bunch of lowlifes like me who wouldn't go to the hospital?"

"Something like that."

After shrugging the unwounded shoulder, the bounty hunter turned and started toward his truck. Shay followed him the few blocks, leaving her car where it was.

When they got to his vehicle, Brownstone pulled the first aid kit out of the backseat and then a spare faded t-shirt out of the front seat.

Shay almost laughed. It was like he'd expected to survive, but lose his shirt. That made her wonder how often he wiped out large gangs.

Maybe it was Brownstone's idea of a fun weekend.

A quip came to her lips, but it never made it out. Instead, she found her attention locked on the man's body. It wasn't that she hadn't noticed his muscles before, but with his shirt off, his rock-hard abs forced her attention despite the weeping slashes in his side and the bullet wound.

The man was the captain of Ripped Town, USA. The savant of six-packs… No, the president of Rippedtopia. Even with the ridges on his face and the odd birthmarks, she could see how a woman could be into him.

Frowning, Shay tried to push the thoughts out of her head. She wasn't interested in Brownstone that way, and even if she were, it didn't matter because the guy was gay. Sewing up wounds was more important than some stupid man's abs and pecs.

She forced her eyes up. "Got any topical anesthesia or anything?" After a few seconds, she added, "Maybe some magical shit?"

Curiosity propelled the question, along with a desire to probe the mysterious bounty hunter's life just a bit more. The more she learned about him, the better she'd be able to put together the puzzle of the truth behind the man.

Brownstone grunted. "I don't like magic much. I avoid it when possible."

"Oh?" Shay found the statement hard to believe, but pissing him off after he'd killed a houseful of Harriken didn't have much upside for her.

"Guns and bandages are more reliable," he continued.

"Not disagreeing, Brownstone." Shay shrugged.

His choice of words struck her as very deliberate. The man was comfortable enough around magical artifacts to help out on raids for Inca zombie wands, and he'd obviously done a lot of work for the Professor. He probably had a few artifacts stashed somewhere for difficult bounties.

"Getting shot hurts a lot more than getting the wound stitched up," Brownstone muttered.

Shay pulled out some disinfectant gel, gut, and a needle from the first aid kit. Her skilled hands soon closed all the bounty hunter's wounds. His face barely moved as she pierced his skin and sutured it.

"There. Can't say you won't scar, though."

"They can join the club. Thanks for the help."

"You're welcome."

Shay stopped her finger from instinctively tracing some of the other scars on his body. They drew her in: each a mark of the man's life-and-death struggles. A person didn't really know who they were until their life was on the line, so Brownstone must have had a hell of a good idea of exactly who he was.

"Hey, you like barbecue?" the bounty hunter rumbled.

"Seriously? You're asking that now?"

"Why not?" Brownstone shrugged. "I'm hungry, and I didn't eat before coming here for my errand." He slipped on the gray t-shirt. "We're not that far from Pork Gods, and they are open late."

Shay stared at Brownstone, trying to process that the man wanted to go for some barbecue right after dishing out that bloodbath in the house.

Then her stomach rumbled. A meal might be nice.

"'Pork Gods?'" Shay snickered. "They think pretty highly of themselves. But, yeah, sure, whatever."

———

Thirty minutes later James sat across from Shay in a booth

at Pork Gods, a gargantuan tray of ribs sitting between them. He'd not said much since placing the order, instead taking the time to polish off a good number of ribs. Killing criminals really did work up an appetite.

James bit into a new rib, enjoying the interplay between the taste of the pork and sauce. He concentrated on verifying the sauce's ingredients. Menus didn't always tell the truth.

Cumin, chili pepper, some black pepper, onions, and tomato, at least. A hint of a couple other ingredients touched his tongue, but he couldn't figure them out. James sniffed the meat but still couldn't identify the mystery components.

An old flat-panel TV on the wall in the corner caught his attention. Some country station was playing a concert video. An Elf woman in a ruffled dress covered in shimmering translucent metallic scales sang, her voice ethereal yet comforting, while steel guitars and fiddles accompanied her. Waves of color pulsed through her dress. Magic or technology—it was hard to tell.

"You like Best of Three Worlds?" Shay asked.

"Huh?"

The tomb raider pointed to the TV with a half-eaten rib. "Best of Three Worlds. Not that I pay that much attention to music, but they have been kind of all over the news. The first Elf to sing country, and all that. Everybody's saying this kind of shit is the future of the two worlds." The mocking tone as she said the last sentence was hard to miss.

James nodded, but then frowned. "Why are they called 'Best of Three Worlds?'" He eyed the Elf woman on the screen. "Oriceran," He held up one finger. "Earth." He held up another finger. "Did I miss something?"

"Oriceran, Earth, and the South." Shay smirked. "Hey, I'm not a country person, so don't ask me. Everyone's saying the woman's going to win a Country Music Award."

"Future of the two worlds, huh?"

Shay shrugged. "Do you believe that? That once everything settles down, it'll be hunky-dory, and we'll be living in magical happy land with all the Elves and wizards and shit?"

James looked around the small restaurant. The few other customers in the restaurant were human, even though there was a decent cross-section of humanity by color, national origin, and age, as could be expected in Los Angeles. Everyone chatted with their friends and enjoyed their barbecue, no tension or concern on their faces.

"People had trouble getting along before any of this Oriceran shit," James said. "People like to divide themselves up. It's not like the Harriken let Mexicans into their gang. Now we're adding magic, along with bringing non-humans over, not to mention...whatever other weird-ass intelligent things they have over there. Like talking statues or some shit."

"Hopeless, then?" Shay didn't sound disappointed as she asked, just curious. "The world ends in blood and fire? James Brownstone headbutting a talking statue as they both get dragged down to Hell?"

James chuckled. That was probably exactly how he'd die.

"I don't know. It's just, you're not gonna be able to bring a lot of people from a very different place to a new place without trouble. Maybe the trouble smooths out and everything ends up better overall...or maybe it doesn't. Not really my problem."

Shay laughed. "You *do* live on Earth, in case you've forgotten."

"Figuring that shit out is above my paygrade. And besides, trouble's good for business."

"That's one way to look at it." Shay chuckled again and shook her head. "So, what do you do when you're not going Old Testament on criminals?"

"I like cooking shows and podcasts, especially on barbecue."

Shay nodded slowly, a glint of amusement in her eyes as the gears in her head turned. "So it'd be accurate to say, you know, that you're a fastidious man who likes cooking?"

James ripped a chunk of meat off his latest rib and swallowed before responding, "If you keep things organized it's simpler for you in the long run, and I like to keep things simple. So yeah."

"Okay, sure. That makes sense."

A ghost of a smile covered Shay's face, but James didn't feel like prying into the woman's mind. He was still getting a handle on her, and her arrival at the Harriken house had taken him by surprise. Shay's mercenary tendencies made sense to him, but he couldn't reconcile that understanding of her with the lack of profit in showing up to help a man avenge his dog.

They lapsed into silence, both working on downing their food, though James' consumption dwarfed Shay's.

"What's your favorite kind?" James said, finally breaking the silence.

"Favorite kind of what?"

"Sauce, of course." James looked as if she'd said the most ridiculous thing he'd heard all day.

Shay's brow knitted in confusion. "You mean, what kind of barbecue sauce is my favorite?"

"Yeah." James gestured with a rib. "We're in a barbecue place. Not exactly a random question."

"Aren't they all kind of the same?" she asked, looking down at her plate.

James grimaced. "Shit, no. Get an education, woman."

The tomb raider grinned. "Sorry if I'm not an expert in barbecue."

"Seriously, it's interesting. A lot of history there, lots of different flavor influences. I like them all, but my favorite are the Carolina-style sauces. Vinegar and peppers are the keys there, though mustard's important in South Carolina-style. Lots of variations though, even at the regional level." James held up a rib. "Pork Gods is more Texas-based. It's okay, but it doesn't hit the spot like Jessie Rae's."

"Jessie's Rae's?"

"It's in Vegas. Best damn barbecue on the planet." James shrugged. "Best damn barbecue on any planet." Oriceran's existence complicated everything, even barbecue.

Shay tilted her head, studying him with a bemused expression on her face.

"What?" James asked.

"Nothing. It's just… I don't know. It's interesting to see the man underneath the living tank."

"What about you? Who lives beneath the snark queen?"

Shay took a deep breath. "I don't like to talk about my past. I've done a lot of things I'm not proud of."

James considered that for a moment. She was cool under pressure, which meant she had probably at least been around some rough characters, but she was also beautiful. The way she'd attacked the man at the Leanan Sídhe suggested deep-seated issues with men.

His stomach tightened as one possibility arose. If Shay had been some sort of sex worker or stripper, it might explain a lot of her attitude toward men and why she didn't want to talk about her past.

Shay put the rib in her hand on her plate and wiped her fingers, then laced them together and rested her chin on them. A seductive smile appeared on her face. "So you can tell me the truth, now that we know each other better."

"The truth?"

"Now that we're not worrying about a job or Harriken or anything else. You like what you see, right?"

James blinked. He was having trouble figuring what the hell Shay was talking about. "'Like what I see?'"

The grinning woman indicated her body.

"What brought that on?" James' gaze dipped for a moment and then returned to her face. Shay was beautiful, no doubt about that, but he didn't get why she was suddenly hitting on him, of all people.

Shay sighed. "I just want you to admit you've been checking me out, Brownstone."

James shrugged. "But I haven't."

"I won't get mad."

"Uh, I still haven't. Not really."

Her smile vanished, replaced by a frown. "Fastidious cooking guy who isn't into me." She nodded and grabbed another pork rib. "Yeah, you're gay."

A few seconds passed before James parsed her comment. She *had* to have said something else.

His eyes narrowed in confusion. "I'm not gay."

"Whatever." Shay cleaned off her hands, pulled her phone out, and tapped a few keys. "I've transferred the money for my part of the meal." She tossed him a wave. "I've got to get going."

"I'm not gay," James repeated.

Shay rolled her eyes. "It's your private life, Brownstone. In the closet, out of the closet—it's not like it's a big deal." She slipped her phone back into the pocket of her jeans and waved.

James watched as she sauntered out of the restaurant, wondering how the hell the conversation had taken such a weird turn.

14

A lison's heart sped up when she stepped into her living room and heard a man's voice from the kitchen. Biting her lip, she pawed around for something useful. A piece of cool metal greeted her hand, and when she slid her hand up it she felt a glass blub. It must have been a lamp from the end table.

She yanked the lamp up, and the cord audibly popped as it pulled from the wall. Her eyesight might have made it hard for her to find a decent weapon, but her energy sight would at least make it easy to spot the intruder.

Heart thundering, the girl crept toward the kitchen, gripping the lamp tightly.

"Yeah, yeah," the man said.

Alison slapped a hand over her mouth to cover her gasp. She recognized the voice.

It was her dad.

"Look, yeah, I understand, Mr. Takahashi," her dad said. "Yeah, I'll get Alison for you. Yeah, yeah." He sighed. "You didn't tell me you needed her—just Nicole."

Nicole. Alison's mom. There it was—her own husband had turned her over to the Harriken. The girl couldn't believe it was a coincidence that two Harriken had tried to snatch her, and now a man named Takahashi was talking to her dad.

How could you, Dad?

Her dad sighed. "If you'd told me at the beginning, I would have delivered her to you." He fell silent for a few seconds. "Okay, okay. We'll all benefit from this. Once I grab her, I'll be able to get that prize. Wait, I think I hear something. I gotta go."

Alison knelt and set the lamp on the ground, then headed toward a wall, feeling along until she found the knob for the closet. She slipped inside, trembling. Her heart was ready to explode.

"Hey, Alison, sweetie!" her dad called from the living room. "You here? I heard you come in and...oh, I get it. I know I didn't call ahead. What, you thought there was some piece-of-shit criminal in our house?"

The only criminal in here is you, butthole. You're a monster.

The girl's hands curled into fists, her anger pushing out some of her fear. She'd assumed her father had had something to do with her mother's disappearance because of the change in his soul color, but now that she'd heard the confirmation, she regretted not charging at him with the lamp.

Alison took a deep breath. She could hear her father as he searched the living room.

"If you're here, you need to answer me, girl. I'm your father, and I deserve your respect. There's only the two of us now, you know."

Thanks to you, jerk!

Alison's lips quivered when her father turned and headed her way. She kept her hands still, afraid that feeling around for a weapon would make noise. Halfway toward the closet, her father turned again and started upstairs.

Seconds stretched into forever before Alison left the closet and rushed toward the front door.

"Alison?" her dad called from upstairs. "Where the fuck are you? Stop playing games."

Alison barreled out the house and up the street, where a rainbow of colors confronted her—people, animals, trees. She glanced behind her. Her dad's dark form was at their front door.

Seeing the energy of living things was great for understanding their feelings, but most people didn't reside in living buildings. Only muscle memory helped Alison navigate as she cut through two yards toward another street, the colors of drivers and people walking up the street acting as beacons.

"Alison!" her dad bellowed in the distance.

Her lungs burned, and her legs ached. Tears streamed down her face as she tried to ignore the pain and the fear. She needed to get somewhere safe, then figure things out.

Alison wasn't sure how long she'd been running when she finally collapsed to her knees, gasping for breath, her stomach churning. The only thing she knew was that she was totally lost.

She forced herself to stand and felt around. She found a cement wall, but the only energy she could see around was small and diffuse. A cat, a few birds. No people appeared to be close by. A little more exploration revealed a wooden fence. She'd been lucky. If she'd kept running in that direction, she would have smacked right into it.

Her home was now off-limits, and the useless cops would just send her back to her dad. They wouldn't believe some teenage girl telling them stories about her dad selling her mom to the Harriken.

Alison wiped away a few tears. It didn't even make any *sense*. Her dad had always been a butthole, but she had thought that he at least somewhat gave a crap about her mom.

"I can't leave here," Alison murmured to herself. The more people around, the greater her chance she would be sent back to her dad.

No. She needed to stay here—wherever the heck that was.

Only one man could help her now.

Alison pulled out her phone, grateful that she'd asked someone to read her the one-use card's number so she could transcribe it into her phone. Her shaking fingers moved across the braille keypad.

The phone rang several times, and she tried to plan what sort of voicemail she should leave.

"I told you that card was one-use," Mr. Brownstone answered, the gravel of his deep voice comforting in a strange way.

"How did you know it was me?"

"You're the only one I've given a card to lately. This better not be for something stupid."

"My dad's back," Alison said, her voice shaking. "I heard him talking to someone on the phone, a Mr. Takahashi.

They talked about my mom. He's planning to give me to this guy. I think the guy must be Harriken."

The bounty hunter grunted. "I take it you're not at home."

"I don't know where I am. I just ran, and now I'm lost."

"Yeah, well, stay where you are. I'll be there soon. Just make sure you keep that card on you until I arrive, or I won't be able to find you."

"Okay, Mr. Brownstone, and thanks."

Alison leaned against the cement wall and slowly slid down. The girl wrapped her arms around her knees and pulled them to her chest, wondering what the Harriken had done to her mom.

Tortured by the thought, she sat there and waited for her savior.

James barreled toward Alison in his F-350, his gaze darting between the road and a small cup in his passenger seat. The needle floating on top of the water shifted direction, so the tracking spell on the card was working.

Lefty the Harriken's words echoed in his mind.

Mount Baldy. There's an old resort that's been converted to a private chalet. The Belmont House. She's there.

James hadn't cared at the time, figuring it was Harriken bullshit that had nothing to do with his revenge, but now everything that had happened since he'd helped the girl out made sense. The first two Harriken hadn't been looking for a new sex slave, they'd targeted Alison after capturing her mother.

The question remained, why? The girl was unusual, which meant the mother might be unusual. The ability to see people's energy might be useful to the criminals, but James had a hard time seeing how it was worth all the trouble—not that the Harriken had planned on having him come to their headquarters and butcher dozens of them.

James grunted. Shit just kept getting more complicated. This was what happened when people got greedy.

The needle changed direction and James took a left turn, cutting someone off. The other driver honked, but didn't come after him.

Smart choice.

Another abrupt change made James jerk the steering wheel. His tires squealed as the truck bounced into the parking lot of an abandoned home and garden warehouse store. He spotted Alison sitting against a wall next to a wooden fence.

James slammed on his brakes and put his truck into Park, then hopped out and jogged toward the teen.

Some middle-aged man with a mustache clumsily hopped the fence, almost landing face-first on the pavement. He reached down and yanked Alison up, while she batted and kicked at him.

The man slammed her against the wall, and she cried out. When she lowered her head, some of her white-tipped dark hair fell in front of her eyes.

James gritted his teeth and started sprinting, which brought him to the pair in seconds. Now that he was closer, he could see a vague family resemblance between the faces.

"Why don't you get away from that girl?" James told the man, menace in his tone.

Alison's dad looked James up and down. "I'm Walt Anderson, and this is my daughter. She's trying to run away, so she can whore herself out. Not gonna let that happen."

James snorted. At least the guy was creative.

"Alison called me and said she was in trouble," James replied. "And the only person causing trouble here is you."

Walt glared at his daughter. "In trouble? What the fuck?" He snapped his head toward James. "I don't know who you are—maybe the guy who wants to pimp her out? Why don't you get your ugly ass out of here before I call the cops on you for attempting kidnapping, asshole?"

James tilted his head back and forth, cracking his neck. "I'm gonna give you a chance to walk away, even though you really deserve to die. Hell, you probably deserve to die more than some of the other people I've killed this week."

The other man's eyes widened, and he paled. "What the hell?"

The bounty hunter took a step forward. "If you turn around and leave right now, I won't kill your ass for being such a piece of shit that you sold your own wife to the Harriken and are planning to sell your daughter."

Alison watched the two men in silence, her cheeks puffy from her tears.

Walt grinned, some of his confidence returning. "You don't know shit, you ugly asshole. I was misled by my wife, so I took care of the situation."

"Misled?"

"It doesn't matter. It's not your business, but if you

know about the Harriken, then you know you should get the hell out of here if you don't want to end up chopped into little pieces and tossed into the ocean."

Alison snickered. "Mr. Brownstone's not afraid of the Harriken."

Walt glared at her. "Then he's as stupid as he is ugly."

James grunted. Mr. Anderson there was really earning his beating.

"Come on, Alison," the bounty hunter snapped. "We're going."

"She's not going anywhere with you." The other man shoved her back against the wall.

"Let me go, butthole," Alison yelled, batting uselessly at his chest. "You're a crappy dad and an awful husband."

Walt backhanded Alison and she fell to the ground, holding her cheek.

"You're not mine," Alison's dad shouted. "Not really. Just because I donated sperm doesn't mean I'll accept that some half-breed like you is my kid. You're gonna grow up to look just like your mother. Shit, I wanted a daughter who'd look like—"

James silenced the man with a punch. The only thing that saved Walt Anderson's life was that the bounty hunter directed him into the parking lot instead of against the cement wall. The man landed with a thud and rolled over the jagged rocks and glass scattered across the cracked pavement.

Walt groaned, holding his face.

The bounty hunter walked over and kicked him in the stomach, sending him flying into the air again.

"So here's my dilemma," James began, narrowing his

eyes at Walt as he squatted beside the man. "You're a worthless piece of shit and you don't exhibit family loyalty, which makes you more of a worthless piece of shit than the average bounty I pull in. Fuck, the Harriken might be assholes, but they never sell out their family members." He knelt by the groaning man. "So I have to ask myself, do I kill you or not?"

"You...can't...do...this," Walt gurgled, blood and a broken jaw making it hard to speak. "The...Harriken...will...kill...you."

James snorted and rose. "The Harriken made a big mistake, so most of the local ones aren't around anymore."

Strangled sobs emerged from Walt. "I just...didn't want...a half-breed. She tricked me."

The bounty hunter lifted his foot. One good kick to the head would finish the man off.

A dark cloud descended on James' heart. He'd lost two fathers, and he knew at least one of them had been a good man. This Walt Anderson deserved to be wiped off the face of the Earth. It'd be easy.

Very easy.

"You get to live, Walt," James said. "But only because killing you would result in a lot of paperwork, and my life's already too fucking complicated. I'd leave Los Angeles if I were you, motherfucker, because next time I see you I might not be in such a lenient mood."

Walt continued sobbing.

James walked over to Alison and pulled her up. "Let's go."

The pair started toward the F-350.

When Alison glanced over her shoulder, the vile

swirling black energy around her father looked denser and darker than before. Darkness had always haunted his soul, but now he'd been consumed by it.

She felt no pity. It would have probably been merciful for Mr. Brownstone to finish him off.

Mom, please be all right.

15

Neither spoke for the next five minutes. James checked a few times to make sure they weren't being followed, but spotted nothing of concern. For all Walt's bluster, he was a chickenshit who wanted to hurt a young girl, not some Harriken enforcer—and even the gangsters weren't much of a threat now.

Alison stared out the side window. "What now, Mr. Brownstone?"

James blew out a long breath. "Not sure, but first things first: we know the Harriken are looking for you, which means I need you somewhere safe with someone I can trust until I can stabilize the situation."

"What do you mean, 'stabilize the situation?'"

"Let's just say I'm gonna convince the Harriken it's in their best interest to leave you the hell alone and give your mother back."

Alison's eyes widened with hope. James didn't want to ruin what little innocence the girl had left by explaining that his form of persuasion would involve another F5 tornado of blood and lead.

And maybe a few grenades.

James cleared his throat. "Like I said, before I go I need to get you somewhere safe."

"Like a secret hideout?" she asked.

The bounty hunter chuckled. "Something like that. My house. I have a new friend I trust enough to have watch you while I go check out some other things."

Shay was the only real possibility. James had a lot of decent contacts, and even people he considered friends, but they all specialized in areas that were great for a bounty hunter but not so great for a bounty hunter who needed to stash a kid.

It wasn't like Father O'Banion or Zoe had any business being around a teenage girl. Hell, James barely had any business being around Alison most of the time.

Taking her to the police would end up with her in the Child Protective Services' custody, if not back with her worthless sonofabitch father.

The cops were honorable men for the most part, but they had to play by the rules—and James didn't. Maybe someone at the church could help him out, but that didn't solve the immediate problem.

James grabbed his phone from the console and dialed Shay.

She picked up the phone after the first ring. "Brownstone, to what do I owe the pleasure?"

"I need your help with something, and I was wondering if you had some time."

"Does this involve killing houses full of gangsters again?"

"Not today, I don't think."

"I love the implied promise." Shay chuckled. "What's up?"

"This is related to the Harriken, just not killing them. Yet."

"Okay, I'm listening."

James slowed to turn onto a busy street. "I originally got the attention of the Harriken because I rescued a teenage girl from two guys trying to snatch her. She was looking for her mom."

"Yeah, and? That sounds like every Tuesday in L.A."

"Well, I've got that girl with me now. Turns out her dad was the one who sold her mom to the Harriken."

"Huh, that's different. Kidnapping a middle-aged mother to turn her into a prostitute or something seems tailor-made to bring down trouble on you, bounty hunter...or the law."

James changed lanes. "There's something more here. Not sure what, but first things first: I wanted to know if you could watch her for a bit while I talk to some people about taking care of her."

"Why me?" Shay asked.

"You showed up because you were pissed about a dog. I don't think you'd sell out a little girl, and I know you know how to use a gun. My other first-line choices include two hardcore drunks."

"So it was me or a drunk?"

"Yeah, something like that."

Shay snickered. "You need better friends, Brownstone."

"We all get the friends we deserve."

Shay muttered something under her breath. "Whatever. Okay, sure, I'll help, if it isn't for too long. I'm not a babysitter. I'm a field archaeologist."

Relief and a feeling of appreciation spread through James, although gratitude toward anyone other than the police or the Church was rare for him.

"Thanks. Meet me at my place. You guys can stay there. I don't think the Harriken will come sniffing around me directly for a while after my little demonstration."

"Okay, Brownstone, I'll do this, but you owe me one."

"Sure." James disconnected the call and tossed the phone back into the console.

Alison huffed. "I'm not a little girl, by the way. I'm fifteen years old."

"Until you can defend yourself, you're a little girl."

The teen rolled her eyes.

Blood warlocks he could deal with. Surly teens were a far more unsettling foe.

***

After Shay knocked on Brownstone's door, she crossed her arms and started tapping her foot. Everything about this was idiotic. She couldn't figure out what weird hold Brownstone had over her that kept making her want to help him.

If she weren't already in the Harriken's sights for showing up at their house the night of the massacre, helping Brownstone protect one of their targets would put her square in the crosshairs.

Still, earning a little trust and a favor from the bounty hunter might be worth it. Plus, she suspected the local Harriken population would nosedive over the next few days.

The door finally opened, revealing the barbecue-loving bounty hunter. He wore his leather jacket on his body and a concerned look on his face.

Brownstone gestured her inside. "Alison's on the couch." He pulled a key out of his pocket. "No reason for you to go anywhere, but just in case."

"Oh, giving me the key to your place already?" Shay winked.

Brownstone just stared at her until she shrugged and sighed. For a man who liked to talk a lot of shit, he could be boring at times.

"I'll be back soon." He headed out the door. "I know you don't like spooky basements, but just so you know—the basement door is locked and sealed for a reason."

Shay glanced that way. "Because it's your Red Room of Pain?"

"It's booby-trapped, too." The bounty hunter shook his head and closed the door behind him.

"Well, at least it's not fucking Inca zombies this time," Shay muttered under her breath.

She continued deeper into the house, taking in the carefully arranged furniture and neatly piled stacks of papers. She spotted Alison on the couch, her hands folded in her lap.

The girl looked up and offered her a smile. She tilted her head, staring at Shay without saying anything. The girl's eyes seemed unfocused, and something about her expression unsettled Shay.

Trauma maybe, from dealing with an asshole dad. Shay could understand that. It wasn't like she'd grown up with the best parents. They hadn't tried to sell her to gangsters, though—she had to give them that.

The field archaeologist reached up and brushed at her cheek. "What? Something on my face?"

"No. I mean, maybe."

"Maybe?"

"It's just that you kind of remind me of Mr. Brownstone."

"How?"

"A beautiful soul covered in a lot of pain."

Shay blinked several times, completely unsure how to respond to that. "Okay. Thanks for that, I guess. Whatever that means."

The girl rose and offered her hand. "I'm Alison, by the way. Alison Anderson." Her smile disappeared. "Though I think I should get my last name changed. I don't honestly know my mom's maiden name. I'll have to ask her once Mr. Brownstone gets her back."

"Yeah, I heard about your old man and your mom. Tough break." Shay shook the girl's hand. "I'm Shay. I'm a work associate of Brownstone's."

"You're a bounty hunter?" Disbelief colored Alison's voice.

Shay shook her head. "No, I specialize in freelance archaeology."

Alison's face scrunched in confusion. "Why would an archaeologist need to work with a bounty hunter?"

"You'd be surprised." Shay winked. "I'm kind of like a mix of Indiana Jones, Lara Croft, and Caleb Rodriguez."

"I've seen a few of the *Ancestor's Quest* movies, but I don't know who Indiana Jones and Lara Croft are."

Shay winced. It was the first time in her life she'd ever felt old, and she was only twenty-seven. Admittedly, she did have a predilection for the classic field archaeologist stories.

"They are cooler than Caleb Rodriguez. I mean, he always uses so many drones and robots. It's just not the same as running from a boulder, watching Nazis melt, or punching sharks."

Alison shrugged. "If you say so."

Innocence clung to the girl in a way that almost turned Shay's stomach. The tomb raider had been around Alison's age when she'd slid into a world of suffering and darkness. Maybe Brownstone could save the girl from a similar fate.

Shay returned her attention to the house. She ran her finger along a windowsill. No dust. *The man dusted his windowsills.* She didn't even do that.

"So have you known Mr. Brownstone long?" Alison asked.

"Nope. Just met him recently on a job."

"He's a good guy, you know. He's saved me twice from the Harriken."

"Yeah, he's okay for a guy."

So much for you only being in it for the money, Brownstone. Helping out little damsels in distress? Where's the profit in that?

A bookshelf caught Shay's attention. Closer inspection revealed three rows of books, the top being cookbooks and the bottom two all being books related to barbecue: history, cooking, chefs, restaurants...that sort of thing.

"*The Case Against Molecular Gastronomy as Applied to Barbeque,*" Shay read. She shook her head. "Man, does this guy like his barbecue!"

Alison tilted her head to the side. "What?"

"Nothing, just... Brownstone's real OCD. I didn't expect that from a guy who... Well, a guy like him."

Wonder if he gets OCD when he's shooting six guys in the face?

Shay turned around and headed to the bathroom to peek inside. Three hand towels hung from a towel rock, all perfectly aligned. The toilet glistened, pristine. The light scent of pine hung in the air.

The bathtub looked factory-new.

"The guy doesn't even have hard-water stains," she mumbled. "I scrub the damn thing, and I *still* have hard-water stains."

Alison rose from the couch and walked over to the bathroom. "What are you doing?"

"We need to leave," Shay told her. "Now."

The teenager's eyes widened. "Are the Harriken coming?"

"No." Shay took a deep breath. "This place is just...too perfect. If we mess anything up, both of us may end up dead. I'm taking you to my place, where a little mess isn't the end of the world."

James knocked lightly on the door to Father McCartney's

office. He had no reason to confess more sins, since he'd already admitted he was going to kill a bunch of Harriken. Talking about killing more Harriken would just waste the priest's time.

"Come in," Father McCartney called.

James opened the door and stepped inside. The priest sat at a weathered oak desk. Other than a bookshelf and a painting of Jesus on the wall, the small brown-painted office lacked any real decoration.

The priest folded his hands in front of him. "I'm glad to see you're...well."

"You mean breathing?"

The priest chuckled. "That too. It's hard for me, you know."

"Hard?"

"I see you not as this powerful man, but as a sad, crying little boy. I don't just fear for your soul. I fear for your life."

James shrugged. "If I do my job, the only people you need to pray for are the victims of the criminals." He sighed. "The situation has become more complicated."

The priest raised an eyebrow. "Is this something I need to hear in the confessional?"

The bounty hunter shook his head. "Nope. I'm not here today to talk about killing people. I need your help."

The priest eyed James for a moment. "I can't be a party to violence, even against the wicked."

James looked affronted. "I'd never ask that of you."

"Then what did you need, James?"

"I rescued a girl from a bad situation. Teenager—only fifteen. She needs a place to stay."

Father McCartney sighed and shook his head. "I'm sorry, but I can't help."

"You can't, or you won't?" James asked.

"I can't. The parish budget is in bad shape, and we can't take any more kids at the orphanage. If I took her in, she'd probably end up with Child Protective Services inside a *week* with a charge of neglect, and I'm guessing she'd end up back in the bad situation you pulled her from."

James scrubbed a hand over his face. "Sh—I mean, that's not good."

"Where is the girl now?"

"Staying with a friend of mine."

James decided that mentioning Alison was staying with a mercenary field archaeologist who probably used to be a sex worker wouldn't help with Father McCartney's blood pressure. The man was already dealing with being confessor to a violent, ruthless bounty hunter and trying to help take care of orphans.

He didn't need any more stress.

"I'll figure something out," James grumbled. "Just my fu —just my luck." He shook his head. "I didn't realize you were having so much trouble with money."

Father McCartney heaved a long sigh. "Money's gotten very tight. Collections are down, and our budget's been slashed. We barely have enough money to feed the few orphans we currently have. I don't know what we're going to do. I've appealed to the bishop for help, but he just keeps telling me that times are rough for everyone."

"I'll bring a tithe for you, Father. Not for Alison—I'll handle her for right now—but for the others. That orphanage... It saved me when I needed it, when I was alone. The least I can do is help you save *it*."

The priest pursed his lips, and he inhaled through his nose. "I don't want blood money, James. Not for an orphanage attached to the church."

"I'd not do that to you, Father. I have non-bounty money I can give. I promise."

"I'll take your word then, James. I may not always approve of what you do, but I know your heart's in the right place."

Considering all the people he'd killed in the last few days James wasn't so sure of that, though he did appreciate that someone still thought he was worth saving. It almost made him think he wasn't a monster.

"Thank you, Father."

16

James sighed as he unlocked his door. Father McCartney had been his only real plan, short of getting the mother back.

The dark truth was that Alison's mother might already be dead or out of the country, despite what Lefty told him. James didn't want to burden the girl with that possibility, but if even he couldn't rescue the woman, he would continue to be responsible for making sure her daughter was safe.

That could wait a few days, at least. For now he needed to show the girl strength, not give her more worries.

When James walked into the hallway connecting to his front door, he didn't hear anyone talking nor any television. Dead silence, other than clocks.

Every muscle in his body tensed. Something was wrong.

No, not-fucking-again.

James ripped his .45 out of his shoulder holster and

rushed forward, but neither Shay nor Alison greeted him in the dining room or living room, alive or dead. The basement door remained secure. Bedrooms, kitchen, bathrooms—all empty.

"What the fuck?" he growled.

His front door squeaked and he spun, his gun up. Time to kill more Harriken.

Shay threw her hands up. "Don't shoot, Brownstone. It's me."

James narrowed his eyes and eased off the trigger. He took a deep breath and holstered his sidearm. "Where the fuck is Alison?"

"At my place. It's safer anyway. I have locks, and security actually made this century. And a panic room."

"Then why the hell aren't you with her?"

Shay shrugged. "Because you're gonna need my help with your next mass-murder spree, big guy."

"Your help?" he asked as he put his pistol back up, locking it into its holster.

She nodded. "Yeah. I know how this whole thing ends. The kid told me about how you're gonna 'persuade' the Harriken." Shay made air quotes at the word persuade. "And we all know that in Brownstone-speak that means you're gonna kill every last one of those motherfuckers."

James grunted. "I might not need to kill *all* of them." He scratched his cheek. "Just most of them."

She just looked at him for a moment. "The point is, sure, you took out that Harriken house, but wherever they're holding the kid's mom is probably a higher-security location. And now they know you're coming. It's gonna be shoot-on-sight, snipers…magic, for all you know.

Maybe one of those talking statues you're so worried about."

Brownstone locked eyes with Shay. "What I did in that house isn't my full strength. I've still got a few tricks to show them. I don't need help. Especially *your* help."

She crossed her arms over her chest. "Can you see behind you, Brownstone?" Shay let out a dark chuckle. "Because that's what it's gonna take not to die. You didn't exactly escape unhurt last time. A bullet through the head or heart will kill even you, Brownstone. Now imagine a .50-cal sniper bullet. Even your skull isn't thick enough to stop that."

James dropped into his recliner. "I don't need some tomb raider to grab the mom while I'm distracting a few guys. If that was your plan, give it up."

He slammed his fist into his palm and twisted it as he looked at her. "This is applied ass-kicking, and I'm the expert here. This isn't about sneaking around, it's about tearing some motherfuckers apart. These guys are an infestation, and I'll be the exterminator."

Shay walked farther into his living room and loomed over him as he sat in the chair. He was almost amused that she was trying to intimidate him, of all people.

"I've got skills, Brownstone. I'm still new at the field archaeology gig. It's not what I trained for all my life."

James snorted as he shook his head, but he eyed her. "Skills? What, like pole dancing?"

Shay's mouth dropped open. Her face reddened, and her eyes blazed murder.

"*What the fuck did you just say?*" she spat, hands on her hips.

James put up a hand. "I know you had a tough life as a stripper or a prostitute or whatever before and I'm sorry for that, but having seen the dark side of people isn't the same thing as doing what I do. It's not enough just to be angry."

Now scarlet-faced, Shay's hands curled into fists. "Is that what you fucking think? That I was a stripper or a prostitute?"

James shrugged and waved at her. "Yeah. You're good looking, you've got issues with men, and you won't talk about your past because you're ashamed. Plus, you keep acting like I should be into you, and you told me I was gay just because I let you know I wasn't."

Shay grit her teeth and looked away, then uncurled her fists and crossed her arms. "This is bullshit." She tried to keep her anger in check. "I shouldn't have to tell you crap about my past."

His voice was stony. "You want to join the party, then I need to know you have the skills to earn an invitation. If you won't tell me about your past, I can't trust you to have my back."

James pushed out of his chair and stood up to stare down at Shay. "Yeah, you're right. One of the Harriken at the house gave up a location. I didn't know what it was for at the time, but now I get it. It's where Alison's mom is. I'm gonna raid the place and rescue her. And you're also right that it's gonna be more dangerous than what happened at the house." He squared his shoulders. "So if you want in, fucking convince me. Otherwise, shut up and go watch the girl."

Shay's mouth twitched for several seconds, and then her eyes dropped. She blew out a huge breath.

"Okay, Brownstone, you win. I'm gonna share my secret with you, although it's something I've tried to leave behind. Just...give me a few minutes to prepare myself."

———

Shay walked into the kitchen and made herself at home. She opened the refrigerator, unsurprised to see everything organized in neat little rows.

"Your house is too damn clean, Brownstone," she called over her shoulder. "Are you *sure* you're not gay?"

The bounty hunter growled from the living room, "I'm not fucking gay, all right? Get over yourself, already."

"Really? This place is too damn clean and organized for a straight guy's house. Whoa, Henry Weinhard Root Beer." Shay resisted the urge to giggle like a school girl. "I haven't had this in years. Best head on a root beer ever."

Brownstone didn't take the bait, which actually argued against her gay theory. Every gay friend she'd ever had liked a good head joke.

Shay let out a sigh. "You're just so..." She shrugged and whispered, "Maybe you're not gay, but I'll find out your secret, Brownstone."

She resisted the urge to grab a root beer. Pulling one out would mess up the symmetric pattern in the container, and Brownstone would probably stroke out when he saw that.

Instead, the tomb raider slowly walked back into the

living room and sat on the couch, folding her hands in front of her.

Brownstone stared at her. "This isn't about my secrets, Shay. It's about yours."

"First off, I was never a stripper or prostitute or anything like that." She shrugged. "I've just always been hot, okay?"

The bounty hunter grunted but didn't say anything.

"Too hot from too young," Shay added.

Brownstone's face softened.

"I'm not from L.A., you know. I'm from out east. When I was fifteen, I caught the eye of a guy in my neighborhood. Nice guy, good looking, also happened to be heavily involved in running dust. The Oriceran shit, not PCP."

Brownstone leaned forward, intent on her story.

"This guy was, you know, really into me. I'm not gonna lie, Brownstone…when you're hot *you* know it and the world does too, so I knew the effect I had on men and boys. I used it to my advantage." Shay shrugged. "When Captain Dust showed up and started buying me gifts, I figured it was no big deal. I'd string him along and then move on, 'cause it wasn't like he could do anything to me. I was only fifteen, right?"

The dark-haired woman took a deep breath and slowly blew it out. Very few people knew what she was about to tell Brownstone. She'd tried to leave her past behind, but it was like the universe wanted to slap her in the face and shake her until she admitted what she was. No one could run from their true nature, it seemed.

"One day I was riding around in Captain Dust's car. He'd taken me out to dinner. I was so impressed with him.

Then he told me to suck him off, and I told him to fuck off."

Brownstone's face hardened. Shay had no doubt about what this man would have done.

Shay gave a long sigh. "He pulled me out of the car, slapped me around, and then told me that he fucking owned me and he could do what he wanted. I told him to fuck off some more, and then he threw me down and told me he was just gonna take what he wanted." She closed her eyes. "For a second, you know, I thought, 'why don't I just let him fuck me, then he'll stop hurting me,' and then I told myself, no, I couldn't do that, because the minute I let one guy do what he wanted, the next guy would as well."

Brownstone nodded slowly but didn't otherwise interject.

"So I told Captain Dust there to get the fuck off or I'd kill him. You know what he did then?"

Shay waited this time. She wanted to hear Brownstone's voice. It'd help anchor her in the present. Her dark emotions swelled and threatened to overwhelm her.

"What did he do?" the bounty hunter asked on cue.

The dark memories continued to pound Shay's mind, and her nails dug into her palm. A few trickles of blood started.

"He pulled out his gun and handed it to me. He slapped me so hard my head bounced off the car, then told me that I was a stupid little cunt who didn't have the balls to kill him. He said that some people had the killer instinct, and some people didn't. He said I would be his forever." Shay stared into the distance, the painful memories feeling as fresh as they had twelve years before. "So I took the gun and shot him right in his dick."

Brownstone blinked and grimaced.

Shay swallowed. "You have to understand, it felt good. Not because I'd shot someone, but because I'd taken control. That was what I hadn't had before. When I was flirting my way through life I'd thought I was in control, but I was really just someone else's toy."

"So you shot him in the dick and let him go to make your point?"

"Would you have?"

Brownstone grunted. "I think you know the answer to that."

"Yeah. I gave him a speech about how I was going to take control, how it wouldn't just be my looks pushing through life, it'd be my skills. Then I shot him until the gun ran out of bullets." Shay sucked in and blew out several deep breaths. "I got rid of the gun, and when people came around asking me if I knew anything, I told them I didn't know shit."

"So you got away with it? None of his friends came looking for you?"

Shay stood up and started pacing. "No, because they made the same mistake you did, Brownstone. They assumed some pretty little thing couldn't be lethal. That I'd make a better stripper or escort or something." She waved a hand. "What I realized after that was that I could kill people and not feel bad about it. That it made me feel powerful and in control, so it grew from there—a life of killing. I was good at it, and people were willing to pay me good money to do it."

"So you became an assassin?"

"No!" Shay gritted her teeth. "I was a killer; cold-blooded, methodical and efficient, but not an assassin. Assassins are pussies who can't be bothered to get blood on themselves. They shoot from a distance. I wanted the people I killed to *know* that I was the one taking their life, to know *I* had the power."

Brownstone's expression had turned stony. She wasn't sure if he was judging her, but she did find it hard to believe that a man who had killed so many people that week would think she'd crossed a moral line.

"But you're not working as a killer now," he replied. "You're trying to be a tomb raider. If you're so damn good at it, then why leave? Why not continue icing people for a paycheck?"

Shay stopped pacing, crossed her arms, and sighed. "Well, one dark and stormy night..." She laughed bitterly. "Yeah, I know...cliché, but that was part of the problem. Let's just say one night it caught up with me—what I'd become. So I walked out of my house as it went up in flames and left my old city and life behind. Too many skeletons for them to be sure I wasn't one of the dead. It wasn't like I'd used my real name for work anyway."

"So you have the skills, I'll give you that, but are you sure you want to help me? If you're trying to walk away from killing, helping me mow down a bunch of Harriken won't exactly set you back on the path of pacifism."

There was no challenge in Brownstone's eyes, just curiosity.

Shay shook her head. "I'm not a killer anymore, but I'm not a pacifist either. I'm like you—I think some people deserve to die. I guess that now I just want to make sure I'm only killing people like that."

The bounty hunter nodded toward the door. "Let's go, then. The longer we wait, the more reinforcements they'll have. First, though, I have to go pick up a few things at the warehouse."

17

S hay stared out the window as the F-350 sped to Brownstone's mysterious warehouse. She appreciated that her partner wasn't chatty. Baring her soul and her past had unsettled her. For that matter, begging to help Brownstone go after the Harriken to rescue the mother of some girl she didn't really know freaked her out.

Trying to make up for being a killer by killing more people? Yeah, great logic there. Plus, helping some weird magic soulreading kid? This won't end well.

Some of Shay's confusion over the Harriken's interest in the girl and her mother had vanished when the girl explained her abilities on the way to Shay's house. The tomb raider theorized the mother had a more refined version of the same ability. A creative criminal group could make good use of such a power.

In the end Alison didn't really remind Shay of herself, despite the age. The tomb raider had never been as naïve or optimistic about people as the girl was. The teen's abilities to see into people's souls might have something to do with that, even though Shay thought that if she could see what most people were like it'd make her more cynical, not less.

Her phone beeped, and she pulled it out of her pocket to check. She grimaced at the on-screen notification, and a few taps brought a loud groan out of her.

"What?" Brownstone asked, keeping his eyes on the road. "Did Henry Weinhard's just go bankrupt or something?"

"I have access to good sources." Shay sighed. "From back in the day. They help me pick up on certain types of information quickly—info about dangerous groups."

"Yeah, and?"

"The Harriken have hired a lot of temporary muscle, including some from outside groups. They are offering ten thousand a head. Another call went out not all that long ago offering extra bonuses if they show up immediately."

Brownstone shrugged. "So what?"

"This means they know we're coming, and probably know we're coming now."

The light commercial areas they'd been driving through had given way to run-down industrial buildings and warehouses. They must have been getting close to their first destination.

"I *did* just kill a bunch of them," Brownstone reminded her. "And Dad of the Year probably called to warn them about me beating him down." His gaze jerked to his side mirror for a second, but then he relaxed. "This is a good thing, anyway."

Shay's brows rose. "A good thing? How are reinforcements and a lack of surprise a good thing?"

"The more guys that are in one place, the less follow-up I have to do if they don't get the point this time."

Shay looked down for a second. "That's one way to look at it."

"You can still back out."

She shook her head. "Nah. Besides, if I don't do this kind of thing every now and again I might get rusty, and you won't always be there to beat up warlocks for me, Brownstone." She put her phone down and looked back out the window. "So let's go find your warehouse."

Shay took several deep breaths to center herself. Maybe her past *would* define her forever.

James pulled the truck into the parking lot of Angels Elite Indoor Long-Term Storage.

Shay eyed the buildings with faint disdain.

The bounty hunter knew exactly what she was focusing on: the cracked and fading paint, the overgrown bushes; even the way the "A" in the neon sign over the place was out. The place looked like shit, and not somewhere that you'd want to keep anything. That was exactly why he liked it.

James reached into his glove box and pulled out a keyring he'd stuck in there before leaving. Thirty-seven very similar-looking keys were on the ring.

Shay laughed. "Got enough keys, Brownstone?"

"No, always need more. Stay in the truck. I'll be right back."

James stepped out of the truck and headed for the door.

He unlocked it and headed into the chilly overly air-conditioned interior, and a walk down a hallway lined with heavily-reinforced doors brought him to his target. He needed three keys to unlock the three heavy-assed deadbolts, after which he stepped into a room filled with printout-filled boxes.

A close examination of most of the papers would have revealed nothing more than copies of posts from now-defunct social networks. They'd already been in the unit when James first rented the room. Why someone had carefully archived posts about three particular pop singers from 2010 through 2022 was a mystery for the ages. Probably some secret Oriceran shit.

James placed his hand on the smooth white back wall and slid it sideways until it felt warmer to the touch. The area around his hand glowed for a second, then with a click a door opened. He sometimes wondered if the people who owned the place would ever realize he'd put in a false wall. Then again, he'd paid his rent for the next ten years, and one of the reasons he'd selected Angels Elite was a tip from a certain unfortunate bounty about their discretion.

There was a dusty shelving unit behind the false wall with several suitcases piled in front of it. Small- and medium-sized boxes occupied its shelves. A safe rested at the other end of the secret space.

James knelt in front of the safe and placed his thumb on a small pad. He held his face steady as his thumb burned. Thirty seconds later, the DNA lock clicked and the safe popped open.

Like a Russian doll, there was a smaller safe inside. A good minute passed as he tapped in a sixty-digit code. His photographic memory relegated idiocy like using '1234' as a passcode to the garbage. The other safe clicked open.

A silver necklace connected to a circular gold and silver amulet rested inside. Three crystals—azure, crimson, and jade—were inlaid into it.

James ran his fingers over the cool crystals. He'd had the necklace on during his first confrontation with the Harriken by a freak chance. When Alison had contacted him, he had been getting ready to take it back to the warehouse.

Oni. Bakemono. Yokai. I don't know what you are, but you're a monster.

James shook his head at the memory of the Harriken's words. The bastard was probably right. If he'd found the necklace on a job it'd be different, but it was something he'd owned since he was a child.

The priest who had taken care of him at first had stored the necklace, thinking it was an important family heirloom that needed to be protected until James came of age. It was only after that man's death that James had gotten the necklace back and realized its power.

"The Granite Ghost." He'd publicized the nickname to intimidate bounties, but it was far closer to the truth than most people realized. Every time he put it on, he couldn't help but feel inhuman.

It had to be all twisted and complicated Oriceran crap. The damn thing's very touch burned until it finished joining with him. James sucked in a breath, not looking forward to having to smell and hear his own flesh sizzling. None of that seemed normal or acceptable, even by Oriceran standards.

Apparently, no one knew why he had the necklace. His parents had died or abandoned him, and then the only man he'd ever thought of as a father had died as well. That suggested there was dark magic behind the item, maybe even a curse.

If magic was real, curses could be real too. Since the necklace might be cursed, James couldn't take the chance of it hurting anyone else.

It was his burden, and his weapon.

The bounty hunter sighed and slipped the necklace into a jacket pocket. He grabbed a small box from the shelf and stuffed it into his other jacket pocket before grabbing two suitcases. He closed the two safes and the secret door before heading out of the unit and locking it again.

It was time to leave the warehouse.

Shay drummed her finger on her leg. She wondered what Brownstone was retrieving from his "warehouse." The man already maintained a sealed secret basement she presumed was filled with a lovely assortment of killing implements.

Movement inside caught her attention. James turned the corner, pulling two suitcases. He pulled a necklace out of his pocket, then removed his jacket and shirt.

Shay took a second to appreciate Brownstone's body and the ink on his arms. She couldn't complain about the view, but the man's decision to suddenly strip confused her. He slipped the amulet around his neck.

Brownstone grimaced as the necklace sank into his

flesh until it was fully embedded, then slipped his shirt back on and grabbed the suitcases.

Shay blinked several times. *I knew you had some sort of magical shit...or is that like some super-secret tech?*

She whispered, her voice floating inside the cab of the truck, "Just who or what the hell are you, James Brownstone?"

———

The F-350 headed east on the I-10, and they arrived at their destination about thirty minutes later. Traffic was light, which helped—every minute they were delayed meant a greater chance of meeting additional reinforcements. James wasn't that worried, but he couldn't be certain the Harriken didn't have secret weapons themselves.

Shay sat quietly staring out the window. James didn't understand the woman completely, but now that he knew her background at least some of her behavior made sense. They'd gone through danger together in Peru, and now they'd both be putting their lives on the line in a situation guaranteed to be bloody. It sure beat falling backward into waiting hands as a trust-building exercise.

James glanced her way. It was rare that someone was quieter than him in most situations. He didn't mind not talking, but a lot of people let their nerves mess with their concentration. A little chatter might loosen Shay up and help her kick more ass.

"I'm surprised they didn't try to suppress the address somehow," he offered.

Shay gave him a shallow nod. "I think they were banking on people not knowing why the place is important. It's too far from town for someone to just randomly wander into it." She grinned. "Of course, God bless the internet, and all that."

"Maybe we should send a little prayer up to Saint Isidore of Seville."

"Huh? I'm not really up on my saints, unless it's, you know, Saint Kitts or Saint Thomas."

"He's the patron saint of the internet."

She eyed him. "No shit? There's a patron saint of the internet?"

James nodded. "Yep. Since 1997, as designated by Pope John Paul II."

"Learn something new every day." Shay glanced over her shoulder to the backseat. "What's in the suitcases?"

"Everything we'll need," James replied. "I call them my go-bags. They are for when I need to kick ass and don't have time to pack everything separately." He frowned. "I'm assuming you know how to use something other than a pistol and a knife?"

Shay chuckled darkly. "If it will shoot or stab someone, I've probably used it at least once. Not a demolitions expert, though."

"Can you use grenades?"

"Yeah, I can use grenades." Shay shook her head. "But remember, this is supposed to be a rescue mission, Brownstone. We can't level the entire place without risking killing the mom."

He nodded. "I know. That's why I didn't bring the rocket launchers."

Shay laughed. "Why am I not surprised you have rocket launchers?"

James pulled into the left lane to pass some family in a sedan who seemed to think that the speed limit was a suggested maximum.

He grunted. "It's just good to have options."

A thin dirt road split off from the highway about fifteen minutes from Belmont House. After about ten minutes on the road, James turned off and drove into a dense cluster of pines.

"We'll hoof it from here," James told her, shutting off the engine. "Otherwise, they may open up with an RPG or something as we drive up."

"Worried about dying right off the bat?" Shay teased.

"Nope, worried about losing this truck." He patted the dash. "I love this thing."

"Ah, yes...priorities. I'll try to make sure, as we lay dying from getting shot a hundred times, that the Harriken promise not to fuck your truck up."

James grinned. "That would be handy."

They hopped out of the truck, and James pulled the suitcases from the back and unzipped them both. One contained boxes of ammo, along with guns and knives. The other contained various types of electronics, as well as with a few tactical harnesses and holsters.

Shay leaned over to grab a harness, and spent a few moments tightening it while James fiddled with a black wristband.

"Jammer?" she asked.

James nodded. "Yeah. Long-range, but doesn't last all that long. I just want to make sure they don't sneak up on us with tactical drones. Too far from the city not to think they might have some of the heavier-duty shit. I prefer fighting people, not machines."

Finished with her harness, Shay eyed the weapons choices before grabbing a couple of semi-automatic pistols and a Steyr machine pistol. She spent the next few moments stuffing her harness with magazines. Efficiency in murder was always a good thing, but for a proper killing, a lady prepared herself for *all* eventualities.

The next few minutes passed in dead silence as they strapped on their weapons and knives. Each ended up also with a handful of grenades, both incendiary and frag.

James pulled out the small box he'd placed in his jacket pocket and opened it. It contained the energy and healing potions he'd picked up from Zoe.

Shay eyed the potions as James slipped them into a pouch on his harness. "For a guy who doesn't like magic, you sure use a lot."

Her eyes held a question. James knew she'd seen him put on the necklace. He'd intended for her to see it. For now, though, he didn't feel like explaining. She'd find out soon enough what the necklace did.

"I *don't* like magic," James explained, "but this is a rescue mission so I have to be a little more careful. I hope it doesn't come down to using more magic than necessary, but I want to be prepared."

Shay slammed a magazine into her Steyr. "I think I'll just stick to shooting and stabbing people."

James chuckled as he seated several throwing knives. "Dead is dead. Don't care how." He stood, taking a final moment to check his load-out. "Just so you know, this is about rescuing the woman. I don't need anyone alive to spread rumors about me this time."

"Got it. Kill 'em all and let God sort 'em out."

I'm sorry, Father McCartney. I got caught up in something bigger than me. If I don't take them down now, it'll only cause trouble later.

James grunted. "Let's go say hello to the Harriken."

She grunted back, trying to force her voice down an octave. "And goodbye."

He led off with a smile playing on his lips.

18

Shay trailed after Brownstone as they jogged toward Belmont House, her heart pounding. People talked about how important it was to remain calm in dangerous situations.

She'd always thought that was bullshit.

A little fear got her heart and adrenalin pumping, which translated to her being faster and stronger. The smallest edge in battle could mean the difference between life and death. It could be difficult to ride the line between fight or flight, but for her it was almost *always* worth it.

Ahead of them, a two-story wooden building nestled comfortably among tall pines. From their check on the internet, Belmont House also contained a basement level. They assumed Nicole Anderson was being kept below.

Cars, SUVs, and trucks lined the paved circle drive leading up to the chalet, from luxury models to junkers.

The pair pushed closer to the target.

Over twenty men lingered outside in the circle drive. Half of them appeared to be Harriken, judging by the swords on their sides. The others were a mixed group of non-Japanese men wearing suits, tactical uniforms, or street clothes with obvious gang colors.

It was like a United Nations of scumbags.

Most of the thugs had pistols or submachine guns in their hands. A few carried assault rifles or shotguns. They were ready to play.

Several drones hovered overhead, their rotors lightly whirring, but from a distance, it was hard to tell if they were armed.

"Looks like they know we're here," Shay muttered. "Some drone probably spotted the truck before we pulled off the road. I would have liked a little more surprise. Not a bunch, but at least some."

Brownstone tapped his jammer band. "If they didn't know before, they'll know now. And sometimes it's better for them to know you're coming and be afraid. They'll make more mistakes that way."

"If you say so."

The drones all halted, hovering in place.

One of the suited men yelled something, and the men in the circle drive spread out.

"Remember," Brownstone rumbled. "We don't need survivors. Do what you need to do. Just don't die."

"Good." Shay flipped her Steyr's safety off. "That makes things easier."

"Let's get closer, and then you lay down suppressive fire," James ordered. "And I'll close and finish them off."

Shay gave him a mock salute. "Aye, aye, sir! And Brownstone?"

"What?"

"Don't get killed by being stupid. Remember, we're here for a reason."

Brownstone grinned. "I haven't been killed yet, and I do dangerous shit all the time."

Shay rolled her eyes. "It only takes one time, dumbass."

They sprinted through the cover of thick tree trunks in a zigzag pattern. One of the thugs shouted.

Time for the fun.

A fusillade of bullets blasted through the woods. Shay offered a burst in return, taking down a poor gangbanger with a pistol. He'd picked a bad day to make an extra buck.

A quick roll brought Shay behind some douchebag's Lexus. Brownstone kept running. Bullets pelted the car and the tomb raider grinned, satisfied that not only did she have decent cover, but some asshole's car was getting shot up. Even if she died, she'd have her revenge from the grave.

Shay popped up and squeezed off a few quick shots. A Harriken with a rifle dropped to the ground, his neck spewing blood. The thugs began to rush toward the other cars for cover, firing wildly.

Brownstone continuing along the circular drive, following the parked vehicles. Bullet after bullet whizzed by him, throwing up dirt and shattering a windshield here or there.

A thug's submachine gun suddenly flew out of his hand, and Shay blinked. The man hadn't let go. It was as if some invisible force had yanked it from his grip. To the man's credit, he dropped his hand to pull out his pistol without any hesitation.

Shay took the opportunity to fire a burst into his chest, and he fell with a scream. She continued sweeping back and forth until she ran out of bullets. No bastards died, but they also didn't risk anymore shots at Brownstone.

Her failure to continue shooting finally sank in, and the thugs opened up on her. The car window next to her shattered, showering her with safety glass fragments.

"Damn it," Shay muttered. "Should have worn a mask." She shook her head to try to get some of the fragments out of her hair.

Now close to several of the men, Brownstone opened fire, his .45 hurling forth its angry contents. Shay took the opportunity to crouch and swap out her empty magazine.

The remaining thugs had bought a clue by this point, and tried to tighten up their formation while continuing to lay down covering fire.

A bullet ripped into the back of Shay's Lexus shield, and her head jerked up. Three men stood on the balcony, firing down at her and Brownstone.

If those guys were better shots we'd probably be dead. Too damn rusty at this.

The old killer instincts now subsumed the field archaeologist. She raised her gun and held down the Steyr's trigger, pelting the three men with bullets.

Two collapsed where they stood and the third bullet-riddled body fell to the ground, landing with a sickening *thud*. She ejected and replaced the mag.

Brownstone charged from his latest cover position, a bright-red Lamborghini. Four men dropped in the blink of an eye, throwing knives stuck in their throats or hearts. The bounty hunter's .45 delivered quick deaths to several others directly after that.

Their screams overlapped.

Shay fired several bursts off to Brownstone's sides, doing her best to pin the thugs down. The concealed enemies stayed down after one man in desert-pattern camouflage took three bullets in the head for his bravery. He didn't even have time to scream before he died.

The sounds of yelling and footsteps from Shay's opposite side forced her to redirect her attention. Reinforcements from the other side of the chalet had arrived, so she needed to distract them before they flanked both her and the bounty hunter.

Okay, as good as time as any to use one of the toys.

Shay grabbed a frag grenade and pulled the pin. "It's been a while." She grinned as she achieved a beautiful forty-five-degree arc. Three...

"Grenade!" one of the men screamed. Two... They all scattered. One!

Most of the shrapnel pierced two Harriken. They'd have to join the Living Battering Ram from the other night in a mass closed-casket funeral. Two other men groaned, having taken more than a few hits themselves. They might not have been killed outright, but they were on their way to dying.

Huh. I forgot how much fun those things could be.

The other reinforcements hesitated, stunned by the carnage—a rookie mistake.

Shay tossed her other frag grenade toward another group, and her incendiary at the back of a gaudy purple SUV being used for cover by some of the reinforcements. The first explosion wounded only a few men, but the second exceeded her wildest expectations.

The explosion ripped into the SUV's gas tank and a

massive fireball erupted from the vehicle, blowing it several feet into the air and setting several men aflame. The shockwave knocked the nearby attackers to the ground.

The burning men screamed.

Shay took advantage of their confusion and pain to dart toward them and give them a fatal overdose of lead. Hell, some of them she was putting out of their misery. She spun on her heel, blasting the groaning and confused men on the opposite side.

The difference between a thug and a true killer was discipline. Being able to inflict violence was easy—it was human nature—but being able to inflict violence when you were terrified and people were dying around you was a much rarer skill.

Shay waited for more victims, scanning the sides of the chalet and looking up for more balcony snipers. Shots rang out, a mix of Brownstone's .45 and the guards' weapons.

Thirty seconds passed, and no more reinforcements showed up. The enemy must have decided that wasting more lives outside was pointless. Shay spun to check on Brownstone's status. Every other man lay dead or dying, except for one Harriken holding a shotgun.

The wide-eyed man backed up slowly as the bounty hunter stalked toward him. He didn't have his pistol out. Shay wondered if he intended to stare him to death.

The criminal threw his gun up and squeezed the trigger. "Die, *oni!*" The shotgun jerked as it released its deadly load.

"No!" Shay screamed as Brownstone took a load of buckshot to the chest.

Why did you get so close, you idiot? You should have been smarter.

She blinked. Something wasn't right—or maybe it was more that something wasn't wrong enough.

Brownstone didn't yell or scream. He didn't jerk or fall. He just stood there with a bored looking expression on his face, like he got shot point-blank in the chest every day and it'd lost all meaning or excitement.

The bounty hunter glanced down at his now-shredded shirt and raised a single finger, wagging it back and forth. "You fuckers keep tearing up my clothes. It's really starting to piss me off."

"Kami-sama tasukete kudasai!" the Harriken screamed.

Shay had no idea what that meant; maybe a plea for mercy or a prayer to God. It wouldn't matter. Whoever ran the universe from beyond seemed to be favoring James Brownstone that day.

The bounty hunter's expression remained unchanged as he reached out and snatched the shotgun from the man. He cracked the gun over his knee like it was a twig and brained the Harriken with the sharp remains of his own weapon. The man's blood splattered on the bounty hunter.

"And you guys keep staining my shirts, too."

The man collapsed to the ground, and Brownstone wiped some of the blood off his face. He mostly succeeded in spreading it around, making him look even more sinister—like some crazed barbarian from the Dark Ages.

Shay stared, agape. She'd seen people killed in many creative ways in her life, but Brownstone's little display was a first.

"Damn," she muttered.

Brownstone turned to look at her, and she gasped. He stared at her with vertically-slit pupils in speckled yellow and green irises, his eyes more like a cat's than a human's. A few seconds later his normal brown human eyes returned.

Shay couldn't muster up anything to say. The man standing before her went well beyond the bounty hunter who'd raided the Harriken house.

Was he even human?

The tomb raider finally managed to open her mouth to comment when she spotted movement from the balcony out of the corner of her eye. She fired without thought, nailing a Harriken holding a rocket launcher, and before she'd even fully turned the man fell backward, his payload blasting into the balcony's overhang.

A fireball bloomed from the area, its roar deafening. The explosion launched a shower of bodies and wood over the circle drive. The remains of the balcony and the room connected to it burned, smoking pouring into the sky.

"Shit," Shay spat. "We're on the clock now, Brownstone —unless not needing to breathe is also on your lists of skills."

"Nah, still need to do that," Brownstone admitted with a shrug. "Let's go get her."

The bounty hunter reloaded his pistol with a fresh magazine and hurried to the front door. Shay ran after him, sparing a last glance at the shotgunner.

You assholes should never have fucked with him.

Eight SUVs sped up the dirt road leading to the chalet, each filled with men in full tactical gear and equipped with assault rifles. In a chaotic world, being a mercenary was a lucrative career choice.

The Grayrock Company prided itself on quick, decisive victories. Taking down a single man with forty trained mercenaries would be easy, no matter how well-trained the target was.

Their commander smiled to himself, pleased at how the job had fallen into their laps just when they were about to deploy again to some desert hellhole filled with barely-distinguishable rebel groups and angry djinn. The company hadn't scored such an easy payday since clearing out those squatting, protesting orphan gangs outside Rio. At least with James Brownstone, they'd maybe get a little excitement. A fight wasn't entertaining without some risk of death.

"Fucking gangsters," the commander said to the men in the vehicle with him. "These pussies are having trouble with one guy. Let's show 'em how real men get this sort of thing done."

Ten thousand dollars each for probably a few minutes of work. What a payday.

Prepare to die, James Brownstone.

19

Ten more men waited inside the building in the foyer. They lasted less than thirty seconds, their screams echoing in the high-vaulted room.

James took a moment to survey the bodies. "Huh, no Topknot Guy. I'm kind of disappointed."

Shay prodded a body with her foot. "Maybe that guy was the local leader, or the head honcho was smart enough to bail when he knew we were coming. Just because the Harriken value strength doesn't mean the guy smart enough to run things is going to stay there and wait for a living tank to show up and kill him."

The bounty hunter grunted. "So I might still have shit to deal with in the future?"

"Brownstone, we've killed a lot of people today, and you killed a lot of people the other day. I think the Harriken have gotten the point by now, and if they haven't, well, they don't have anybody left. They'll probably start sending you a fruit basket on your birthday."

The acrid smell of smoke from upstairs filled James' nostrils. "We've got to get moving. I'll take point."

He was out of .45 mags at this point, so he pulled out a 9mm. Shay had also run out of ammo for her Steyr, so she readied a pistol.

The smell of smoke grew stronger. Belmont House would die in flames, and something about that idea soothed James. He wasn't sure what pissed him off more about the Harriken: their basic thuggery or their arrogance.

They'd had many chances to deescalate the situation, but they chose to create more trouble each time. Belmont House's burnt ruins would be a monument to their idiocy.

James hurried down the hallway. They couldn't spend too much time fooling around now that the house was on fire, even if it remained contained to the top floor for the moment.

A minute of searching revealed the basement door. No other enemies confronted them, making James wonder if they had successfully killed everyone in the building. The thought disappointed him.

Unlike at the house in the city, this door wasn't even locked or reinforced. It'd become obvious that the Harriken hadn't believed—until the attack on the house—that anyone would dare besiege them in this remote location. A little less arrogance might have saved at least some of their lives.

James nodded to Shay, raising his gun. "Three...two...one!" He threw open the door. No brave enforcer stood on the stairs ready to gun them down or stab them.

The pair rushed down the stairs. The stench of blood hung heavy in the air.

Unlike the storage room at the Harriken house, the Belmont House basement appeared to have once been some sort of torture room. A single table and carts filled with bloodied blades, screws, and pins filled the center of the room. One cart even held a few lead-acid batteries with thick alligator clamps. It was everything a sick-ass psychopath might need.

The elaborate twisted-metal light fixture hanging overhead lacked light bulbs, leaving a dim standing lamp in the corner the only source of light.

An ebony-skinned woman with long bright-white hair lay on the table, her hands and feet secured by ropes. She wore only a torn dull-green hospital gown. Jagged lacerations, bloodstains, burns, and abrasions covered her body, arms, legs, and face. The fingers on one of her hands were bent at extreme angles. There was some sort of metal sheet around her chest.

James' stomach tightened. Killing someone in a fight was one thing.

Torture was another.

He let out a low growl, wishing God would restore the men outside to life so he could kill them again.

"Nicole Anderson?" James asked, slightly confused. He could see a facial resemblance between Alison and the woman on the table, but she was as dark as night, unlike her daughter.

The woman slowly turned her head. "So much screaming. You killed them all, I hope?"

"Yeah, we killed them all. Some of them may take a while to die, though."

"Good. Why? Are you here for what they sought?" Nicole stared at him, her expression weary.

"I'm here because a girl needs her mother." James pulled out a knife. "I helped your daughter out the other day." He sliced one of the ropes. "Because she helped me with my dog. The Harriken tried to take her, and I made them pay for that. Things escalated from there." He made short work of the other ropes and the metal they had her wrapped in. Magical suppression, maybe? "And so now a lot more Harriken are dead. Things just got...complicated."

"Is Alison safe?" Nicole weakly pushed herself into a sitting position. "My husband sold me out, and I know he was targeting her too." She sighed and took a deep breath. "I hoped that his twisted mind might at least show some mercy toward his own daughter."

"Alison's safe. We've got her stashed somewhere the Harriken can't find her." James rubbed his chin. "And I had a discussion with Walt about proper respect for his wife and child. It ended with a broken jaw, and a warning from me that he'd better get the fuck out of town or he would be dead."

Nicole nodded slowly, a pleased look on her face. "He loved me once, I think, but still... What he's done is unforgiveable. Please promise me you'll kill him should you get the chance?"

"I gave him my warning. Especially after seeing this shit," he nodded at her, "if I see him again, he's dead."

"You have no idea how that quiets my soul." Nicole groaned. Her damaged hand glowed for a second, and the fingers moved back into their proper position. Several of her wounds sealed themselves.

Shay kept her attention on the stairwell and her gun up. "I don't get it. What's worth all this bullshit? Can you see souls like your daughter? Did they want to use you as a lie detector or something?"

James shrugged. "Does it fucking matter? We can do the Q and A later. This place is on fire, remember? Let's just get her the hell out of here."

Nicole stared at James, not saying a word. He shifted under her gaze, uncomfortable. She coughed some blood into her hand.

"Shit." The bounty hunter reached into his pocket and pulled out the healing potion. "This is magic. It'll help you." He held it out. "Best potions witch in Los Angeles made it."

Nicole wrapped her hand around his and closed his fingers. "Was this potion made for you?"

"Yeah, whatever. You can pay me back later. You're not gonna make it otherwise."

"You don't understand. It won't work. If anything, it'll probably make things worse."

James winced, remembering all the trouble Zoe'd had getting one to work on him. That was one of the reasons he hated magic so much. It promised easy solutions to complicated problems, but in the end you could never rely on it when you needed it. Everything just ended up more complicated than before.

James scrubbed a hand over his face, trying to think of what they could do.

"What's your name?" Nicole asked quietly.

"James Brownstone."

She smiled at him, looking him in his eyes, Her Oriceran face was otherworldly. "Thank you, James Brownstone, for all that you have done to aid my daughter. I can die now, secure in the knowledge that she's safe, but there is something you should know."

Shay called over her shoulder, "Like my friend said, the house is on *fire*."

Nicole smiled sadly. "I'll be dead soon anyway. You need to understand what I'm going to tell you."

James shook his head. "What the fuck is going on?" He looked at Shay before turning back to Nicole.

"My legacy is a *wish*," Nicole said softly. "I ran from my family responsibilities and duties on Oriceran, but it did not change the truth that those in my line are bequeathed a wish."

"A wish?" Shay turned around, surprised. "You mean...like an actual 'I wish I were rich' kind of wish?"

James glanced at Shay, then back to Nicole once more.

"Something like that. Magic is more powerful and wild than you humans understand." The dark woman leaned forward, her long white hair covering her face. "I wanted to come here and live a simpler life, so I used my magic to disguise myself, took a human husband, and bore a half-human child. But with the truth of Oriceran coming out and my heritage becoming more obvious with the flow of magic each year, my husband figured out the truth. That was fine, since I'd always wanted to tell him anyway, but then I made my true mistake."

"Your true mistake?" James said.

Nicole nodded. "I told him everything, including that I had a wish and was saving it for our daughter. Foolish me,

I thought he'd understand." She inhaled. "I can give the wish to another, but it has to be done willingly. I refused Walt's request. I knew he would not use it well, but I never suspected he'd partner with such scum to betray me."

She gestured to the table. "They tortured me to try and force me to give them the wish, but I am two hundred and twelve years old, and I am a princess of an ancient and dangerous line. These maggots could not have broken my will if they'd had another century to do so. I was prepared to die to deny them what they'd steal from my child, despite the pain."

James stared at the woman, processing everything Nicole explained. This whole thing had started with him looking for Leeroy. Finding some centuries-old Oriceran princess was about the last thing he'd expected to come out of that.

So much for KISS.

"Damn it," Shay muttered. "I'm hearing movement upstairs, Brownstone. We need to move *now*."

Nicole slid off the table and slowly made her way toward the stairs, passing James.

James grabbed her arm. "What are you doing?" He leaned over. "You stay here. We'll deal with the assholes upstairs, then we'll figure something out. I may not know much about healing and magic and shit, but I solve problems." He jerked a thumb upwards. "These types of problems."

Nicole shook her head and smiled grimly. "It's too late for me. Too much of my magic has been expended trying to save my life."

"Can't we take you to some Oriceran healer to help you?"

She shook her head. "No. To keep myself alive, I've been feeding off my own life force. All things have a cost. At this point I'm only delaying the inevitable, but I have enough magic left for one important task."

"What's that?"

Nicole's expression and eyes hardened, and he could see the demons that her kind probably played with as kids behind her visage. "*Vengeance.*"

James released her arm. If there was one motivation he understood, it was vengeance. "We've killed two housefuls of Harriken already."

"Do you think my vengeance too much, human? I would destroy these men over and over if I had the ability."

Shay snorted. "Brownstone killed dozens of people for murdering his dog. Trust me, he's not judging you...and I've got my own past."

Nicole's eyes glinted in satisfaction. "Then you understand what I must do, and *why* I must do it."

James nodded. "I just wanted you to know that no matter what happens, they've already felt pain. And I hope they feel more." He glanced at Shay. "We'll back you up. These fuckers will kill us anyway, and I don't mind going after a few more after what I just saw."

"No. I may not be able to fully control myself when I do what I must do. You have killed my enemies and saved my daughter. I'd not wish to kill you by accident."

Shay stepped away from the stairs after James reluctantly nodded.

Nicole padded toward the stairs, something elegant and

lethal in her movements. "These men will learn why you do not earn the wrath of a princess of the Drow."

James looked at Shay and she shrugged, apparently just as clueless as him what that meant.

"Do not come up if you value your lives." Nicole went up the stairs.

Nicole glanced back down the stairs at James and Shay. The humans hadn't even realized what they'd done when they severed the ropes and *emtal*. She still didn't understand how the lackwit Harriken had found rope with such a powerful magic-sapping enchantment. If it hadn't been for her husband's betrayal and the damnable bindings, she could have made the men pay a while back.

The Drow emerged at the top of the stairs with bloody vengeance on her mind. She'd fled from what she'd thought was a dying world, armed with a desire to leave duty behind; to do nothing more than live the simple life denied her on Oriceran. The dream hadn't been born of greed, so to be denied its continuation now, after so few years, seemed cruel.

Love. Marriage. Contentment. She'd found it all on Earth, and then the greatest joy ever was given her: Alison. In her centuries of life, she'd never felt more satisfied in giving herself to another without concern for power or politics.

Walt had let his avarice destroy all that, aided by violent and petty men with myopic vision. These short-lived insects desperately craved power they wouldn't even be able to control, and from what James had told her, it'd already cost most of them their lives.

The thought saddened her. Her soul burned for vengeance. She wanted to strike back at the men who'd tortured her and destroyed her life. She could only pray that James would find her husband again and make him suffer for betraying his sacred vows.

Till death do us part.

For a short-lived creature like a human perhaps that it didn't seem like much, but to a being such as Nicole with a lifespan of centuries, such words meant more than any prayer to any god, human or Oriceran.

"Alpha and Beta squads in position," called a man from down the hallway. "We have no eyes on target. I repeat, we have no eyes on target. No survivors located. Brownstone slaughtered them."

Nicole narrowed her eyes. Someone *had* come. The men didn't sound like Harriken, but that didn't make them innocent. Their mere presence in this house of horrors suggested culpability.

The Drow rested against a wall, her arm cradling her stomach. Sadness crushed her. She would never see her daughter again in this life.

Alison's laughing face filled Nicole's mind. Her first birthday. Her first day of school. Her first trip to Happy Magic Land Amusement Park.

Blow out your candle, honey, and make a wish.

The wish. They'd all wanted the fucking wish. She'd given up wealth, power, status, and even the use of most of her magic to ask for less, but these damned men who were wealthy and powerful on their world wanted *more.*

Why couldn't you have just been happy with me, Walt?

Nicole shook her head, remembering his last words to her: *It's not wrong to prefer people who look like yourself. You lied to me. Our daughter's going to get darker too, isn't she? She won't even look like me. She'll just be some disgusting half-breed.*

"Will confirm, Command," called the man from before, his voice easily heard through the whispers in her mind.

The Drow princess took several steps down the hallway, her movements all but silent. The buzz of radios and the heavy bootsteps drew her toward the voice. Her heart thundered, desperate for her vengeance to take a physical form.

You think you know violence, humans? You think you know death?

YOU KNOW NOTHING!

A man in uniform turned a corner, rifle in hand. The uniform looked military, but a patch caught her attention: Grayson PMC Services.

"I've got a target," the mercenary said. "Target appears to be wounded. Not Brownstone."

Three more mercenaries hurried toward him, all keeping their guns aimed.

Nicole took a few deep breaths, and a faint burning sensation spread through her body. She didn't have much time. But despite her rage, she needed to make sure her targets deserved it. If the appearance of James Brownstone proved anything, it was that good humans still existed on Earth. She'd at least take the time to establish if these new arrivals were his friends or his foes.

"You don't seem like Harriken," she asked, eyeing their uniforms. "I would consider letting you leave here with your lives, provided you're no threat to James Brownstone."

The man's face tightened. "Sit down, shut up, and put your hands in the air." He nodded to the other men. "We'll ask the Harriken what to do with her later." His gaze lingered on her legs for a second. "Maybe we'll have a little fun first."

Nicole inhaled deeply. "You threaten Brownstone and you do the bidding of the Harriken? And you're men of base appetites. I appreciate you explaining the situation. Thank you."

The man's face scrunched in confusion "'Thank you?'"

"Yes. I was worried for a second that I wouldn't be able to taste any vengeance, but *you'll do nicely.*"

"Just shoot the bitch, man," said one of the other mercenaries. "We'll say Brownstone did it. We don't have time to fuck around with her."

A shadowy nimbus of energy surrounded Nicole, and her eyes turned solid black.

"What the fuck?" the mercenary shouted. "This is Alpha Four. We have a magic user of unknown ability. I repeat, we have a magic user of unknown ability." He swallowed, keeping his gun trained on her. "Great intel on this op. Fucking Harriken."

Nicole tilted her head. To her eyes the men glowed

now, their life forces pulsing around them. "How many people have you killed, Alpha Four?"

"Stand down, woman, or I will kill you. This is your only warning."

"Have you killed innocents? Children?"

The mercenary snorted. "I kill whoever I get paid to kill, you freak bitch."

Nicole sighed. "Then you have no honor to salvage."

The Drow was a blur as she ran along the wall parallel to the floor, her magic anchoring her. Bullets blasted through the hallway, narrowly missing her. A blade of dark energy extended from her wrist, and she leapt from the wall. Alpha Four couldn't even scream as the shadow blade slammed into his throat.

Nicole somersaulted off his body, a glowing scarlet tendril connecting the shadowy energy field around her to the man. The tendril pulsed brighter as she drained his life.

"Humans don't have much life force," Nicole lamented, shaking her head. "It's a wonder you spend so much time trying to waste it."

The other three men backed up, their eyes widening in fear. They sprayed bullets at her, but they bounced off the shadow armor surrounding her body.

"Target is immune to bullets," a mercenary yelled into his mic. "I repeat, target is bullet-immune!"

Gray smoke hung near the ceiling now. She didn't know how long it would be before the hungry fire crawled down the stairs in search of more prey, but she wouldn't let these Harriken-funded killers escape with their lives.

Nicole's shadow blade disappeared, and she held up

both hands. "Rejoice! Your friend gave his life so that you could experience a death few humans have."

The men turned to run. Three dark orbs burst from Nicole's hands and blasted into each man. A smokeless fire surrounded them, charring them, their flesh devoured as they fell. They collapsed to the ground, screaming in agony.

The Drow princess stepped toward the dying men, tendrils extending from the energy nimbus to implant into each and feed what remained of their lives into her armor. She used the rest of her life to form two jagged shadow blades, one for each hand. She marched toward the living room, the fire within her body building.

She sucked in a breath and gritted her teeth.

Just a little longer.

Dead Harriken and other thugs covered the floor, their blood staining the carpet. She admired the straightforward brutality of James Brownstone and his associate, even as she regretted not having been the one to have killed these men.

She had left her people, but their training had not left her.

Twelve mercenaries popped up from behind bullet-riddled cars outside, and their weapons came alive. Bullets splintered the wood and shattered the windows, but pounded uselessly against the shadow armor flowing over Nicole's body.

The Drow rushed the door, her movements again blurring. She decapitated a man before slowing, and his head hadn't even hit the ground when she stabbed her blade through the second's heart. She spun, her other blade cutting another man in half.

One mercenary, seeing his impending doom, pulled the pin on his grenade and tried to tackle the Drow princess. She impaled his hand on the blade and waited as tendrils sucked the life out of him and his friends. The grenade exploded, doing nothing more than annoy her.

The din of eight rifles firing full auto at near point-blank range overwhelmed the area, and casing after casing clattered to the ground.

"Fuck fuck *fuck*," shouted a mercenary, the gun in his hand battering his arm as he fired round after round. "Just die already, *bitch!*"

Fiery pain spiked through the Drow's body. The bullets continued to bounce off her shadow armor, but she was nearing the limits of her already broken magic. She'd fed on her own life to bring herself to this point, and now the bill was due.

Nicole swept both arms wide, and dozens of tightly-woven dark energy ribbons shot from her arms and blasted holes through the chests of the nearby mercenaries. They collapsed to the ground within seconds of each other, moaning through the last few moments of their lives. She drank in what little life they still had before they died.

More mercenaries rushed from either side of the house, a couple dozen or so. None fired.

"Have you learned you cannot oppose me?" Nicole shouted.

One man rushed right at her with a knife in his hand. She laughed.

"I honor your bravery, soldier."

The weapon slammed into her stomach and she gasped, coughing up blood.

"You like that, bitch?" the man snarled. "That's a little something I picked up in Cairo. They said it's good for killing djinn. Looks like it's good for killing witches, too."

"I...am...no...witch." Nicole grabbed his throat, and the man gagged and shuddered as his life flowed directly into the Drow. She yanked out the enchanted blade and tossed it to the ground, not even bothering to redirect any magic to the stomach wound. Fire burned through her veins now, and she'd be dead long before she could bleed out.

A strong pulse of energy propelled her high into the air and four wings of shadow sprouted from her back, keeping her aloft. Six of her shadow spears took out some of the mercenaries before they realized what was attacking them.

"Light her up!" shouted one of the men. "Everything you've got."

The sky came alive with bullets and rocket-propelled grenades. Explosions blasted in rapid succession, filling the sky with smoke, flame, and shrapnel.

For a few seconds, the smoke lingered, and no one spotted the Drow.

"We got her," someone yelled. Several men cheered.

Nicole flew out of the smoke, her eyes flashing and her white hair flowing in the wind. "Too weak." She launched an orb into the man who'd made the false pronouncement, and he collapsed in dark fire. The mercenaries held station long enough for her to burn six more before they broke and ran in all directions.

The Drow princess pulled the energy from her rings and slammed her hand into the ground, and a nova of dark energy blasted from her. All but one of the remaining mercenaries screamed, collapsing to the ground. They twitched, coughing up blood and convulsing.

Nicole took a deep breath, trying her best not to collapse. The burning sensation from before had intensified.

The single surviving mercenary dropped his gun and walked toward her, his hands up. The man's weathered face and graying hair suggested this was far from his first battle. She assumed he was in charge.

"What are you?" he asked.

Nicole stared at him. "I am a princess of the Drow. I gave your men a chance to leave, and they threatened murder and rape."

"I'm sorry for my men's actions." The mercenary commander slowly lowered his hands. "But it seems like they've paid, and then some."

"And you're not angry with me for killing your men?"

"Maybe I'm just accepting the cards I've been dealt. Doesn't matter if I'm angry or not. I can't win against you."

Nicole looked him up and down, curious why he was still alive. "You survived. How impressive."

"I've got an instinct for survival." The mercenary patted his chest. "I've got something on under here that helps protect me. Bullets aren't enough anymore in this world. Funny how things have changed since I started."

He shrugged. "Look, you killed my men, but that comes with the job. You're more powerful than a lot of the weird shit I've seen. I can help make you wealthy beyond your dreams." He nodded toward a dead man. "You like killing people? Gets you off? Lots of people out there who need killing, and lots of people willing to pay for that."

The Drow princess let out a cruel laugh. "I left behind wealth and power for love. I've no interest in your petty offer."

"Everyone has a price."

"Perhaps." Nicole sauntered up to the mercenary leader. "I have one question for you."

"Sure." The mercenary commander licked his lips, the fear still heavy in his eyes.

Nicole's eyes blazed with a feral hunger. "Does your trick work with bullets?"

The mercenary shook his head. "Good old Kevlar for that."

"Interesting." She held up her hand. A shadow arm shot out and snatched a rifle from the ground, bringing it to her hand.

The man held up his hands. "No, wait. We were just hired to take out Brownstone. We could make some sort of de—"

Nicole pulled the trigger, and his head exploded.

The Drow princess collapsed to her knees, coughing up blood and trying to keep her eyes open. Infernos burned in every cell of her body now, and tears streamed down her cheeks.

"Oh, my sweet Alison. I tried so hard not to leave you alone."

21

Shay paced at the bottom of the stairs. "I don't hear any more gunfire or screaming." She shook her head. "We should have been up there, not sitting here in the basement of a burning building like some dumbass JV kill squad."

James shrugged. "When someone gives you a warning like that, you listen."

"And what if they killed her?"

"She was already dying. You heard it, and if they did, the answer is simple."

Shay put her hands on her hips. "Oh? Enlighten me with your great wisdom then, Brownstone."

"The answer is, we kill the people who killed her."

"Okay, fair enough. I like that plan."

James grunted. "Anyway, you're right. Whatever happened is over. Let's go."

They pulled their guns and hurried up the stairs. Thick smoke now hugged the ceiling, and the crackle and hiss of the fire grew louder. Shay coughed a few times.

"Yeah, leaving's definitely a good idea," she muttered.

The pair traveled down the hallway to where four new bodies lay on the ground.

"Grayson," James commented as he viewed their patches. "I know these guys. Mercenaries. Real scum. Never really had a run in with them since we hang in different circles, but I've known people who have. They'd shoot their own mothers for money."

"Yeah, I've heard of them." Shay's nose wrinkled as she gestured to the three crispy corpses. "Smells like burnt pork."

The bounty hunter's gaze shifted from the burn victims to the other man, who had a clean hole in his throat. The Drow woman had been tortured for days, and still took out trained mercenaries with ease. If she'd been killed, it hadn't been in this hallway.

James and Shay rushed toward the front door, both coughing. They paused for a moment to search for live enemies, but seeing only bodies, they stepped outside. It took them a moment to separate the people they'd killed from the mercenaries Nicole had destroyed.

"I pity the cops who have to investigate this shit," James remarked.

Shay shrugged. "They'll play it off as some sort of gang war gone bad, or maybe even a gang summit gone bad. When it's scumbags killing scumbags, it's not like the cops try that hard. I think they think that every dead gangster means the world's a safer place."

"What the fuck?" James said, looking at half a body. It took him a few seconds to realize the man had been cut in half and not flayed on one side. He shook his head. "Can't say I've seen that before."

Shay leaned down and poked her gun through a hole in a dead mercenary. "If this is what she does when she's weak, I'd hate to see what she's like when she's at the top of her game."

Both turned at the sound of a soft moan. They rushed to the source and found Nicole kneeling on the ground, blood covering the front of her hospital gown.

James wasn't sure if it was her blood or that of the nearly-decapitated body lying in front of her. A quick inspection of the rank insignia suggested he was the commander of the unit—yet another man who'd picked a really bad day to try to make ten thousand dollars.

"You okay?" the bounty hunter asked, reaching down.

Nicole put out a hand and let him help her stand as she stared at the burning Belmont House. The fire had engulfed the entire structure now, the conflagration sending a thick plume of smoke into the sky.

Part of the roof collapsed with a loud groan.

"Glad we're not in there anymore," Shay mumbled. "Be pretty weak to die in a fire after going through all that."

Nicole smiled at James and spoke softly. "I wish I'd married a man like you."

James grunted. "Trust me, you wouldn't wish that if you knew me that well. I don't think I'm marriage material for you or anyone else on this planet or Oriceran."

"I know that my daughter's own father was prepared to sell her to criminals for power, and you, a man who didn't even know her, *protected* her."

James shook his head. "I'm paying my debts. She helped me find my dog when he was missing. There's nothing more here. I pay my debts so I don't owe anyone. I like my life simple."

"You told me about all the men you've killed." She waved a hand around, "You're trying to tell me this is just about paying a debt concerning your dog?"

He looked at the carnage around them and turned back to her, running a hand through his hair. "Like I said, things got complicated. I was trying to simplify them."

Nicole weakly laughed. "Most men do everything they can to declare their honor and glory to the world. Are you so afraid of admitting you're a good man, James Brownstone?"

James snorted. "I killed a lot of people this week. 'Good man' would be stretching it. Some might say I'm okay or useful, but I don't think anyone would say I'm a *good* man."

"James, I've lived on Earth for decades, and I still find human morality strange. You worry over the strangest things, while letting the meaningless and trivial things distract you."

"Probably shouldn't have moved to L.A. if you wanted a place with understandable people who aren't easily distracted by meaningless trivia," Shay interjected.

James shot her a harsh look.

She shrugged, putting up her hands. "Just sayin'."

Nicole sighed. "It's taking all my control to keep my power from consuming the last of me, but I will die satisfied, knowing that at least I saved you from these fake soldiers."

James glanced at the dead mercenary company commander. Grayson had access to some heavy weaponry, and unlike the Harriken, they had hardcore battlefield experience. He wasn't so sure he could have escaped unscathed from an encounter with them, let alone brought Shay through.

"We can still take you somewhere," he whispered. "It doesn't have to end this way."

She shook her head. "No, it ended the second Walt betrayed me. There's nothing anyone could do, even back on Oriceran." Nicole wrapped her arms around herself and took a shuddering breath. "I need you to take care of my daughter, the new Princess of the Shadow Forged. I've harmed her by keeping her heritage from her, and I just hope she'll forgive me."

"I… Shit." James rubbed the back of his neck. "All she wants is for you to come back."

Tears leaked down Nicole's face as she shook her head. "I know, but there's nothing I can do. My time is done, and I must see to her future. And that's why *I need you*."

James didn't know what to say. It wasn't like he was prepared to tell this dying woman that he wouldn't take care of her daughter. After everything she'd gone through, the betrayal and the torture, she should at least be able to go to her death without worrying about her daughter ending up in some poorly-funded group home.

James sighed. He'd figure something out. Maybe Father McCartney could help after all, or at least point him in the direction of someone other than social services. Los Angeles wasn't some stupid village. There had to be a good solution that didn't involve James playing at being a foster father.

"I'll make sure she's taken care of," he finally said. "You have my word."

"Oh, I know that she'll be taken care of, James Brownstone. I can see it in you."

"Is...there anything we can do? I could call a priest to give you last rites. I don't know if it works over the phone, but it's something. Or is there someone else we can call?"

"It's okay. What I believe is...quite different than you, even if ultimately it all goes back to the same source."

Frustration boiled up in the bounty hunter. It wasn't supposed to end this way. He'd armed himself—even using the damned necklace—and killed a lot of people to rescue her, but she wasn't going to make it. He'd long since stopped believing in the fairness of the universe, but it didn't make him any less angry.

Doubt gnawed at him. The Harriken at the first house had given him the location, but the bounty hunter hadn't acted on it right away, thinking it had nothing to do with him. His jaw tightened as he wondered if Nicole could have survived if he'd realized the importance of the message right away.

Fuck. It doesn't matter if I want to say it's not my problem. The least I can do is make sure Alison is taken care of, one way or another.

The Drow princess placed a gentle hand on his shoulder. "I can see that this worries you, but don't blame yourself. You've punished the people who have done this to me, and you saved my daughter. That's all I could ask or hope for in this horrible situation."

The bounty hunter averted his gaze, no quips coming to his mind for once.

Nicole looked at Shay with a sly smile. "I see so much now that I'm using my full abilities once more."

Shay frowned. "Like?"

She smirked. "Even now your heart is choosing, and there isn't a damn thing you're going to be able to do about it when it is finished."

The other woman narrowed her eyes. "Not to be rude, but what the hell are you talking about?"

James shot Shay another glare. The least they could do was be polite during the last few minutes the woman had on Earth.

Nicole stepped toward him, though she kept her focus on Shay. "I'm going to make it easier for you to choose." A mischievous smile appeared on her face.

Total surprise was rare for the bounty hunter, but that was the only way to describe his reaction when Nicole threw her arms around his neck and stuck her tongue down his throat, giving him a kiss that made his damn skin feel like a lightning bolt had just hit nearby.

Indecision paralyzed him. He couldn't just push her off, given that she was on the verge of death, but the woman was trying to suck his tonsils out. Shay loudly cleared her throat in irritation.

How the fuck did I end up in this situation?

Nicole's hold on him slackened, and she collapsed. James grabbed her before she hit the ground and she shuddered, her eyes unfocused. Asking her about the kiss seemed inappropriate given the seizure wracking her.

"Come closer," she said quietly. "I have something to tell you."

James lowered his head near her mouth. "What? Is there anything I can do?"

"I've transferred the wish to you," Nicole whispered.

James' eyes narrowed. "What the hell?"

She continued whispering, touching him gently on the chest. "I transferred the wish willingly and freely through the kiss. I've entrusted it to you for my daughter. Now you are bound to her."

James furrowed his brow. "You don't know me. I'm a bad man. The only thing that has ever truly loved me was a dog, and I couldn't even keep him from getting killed by the Harriken. I'm a monster, and the only reason I'm tolerated is because people need me to fight bigger monsters. You can't trust me, and you *shouldn't* trust me."

"If you believe that then you're a *fool*, James." She weakly patted him on the chest. "I can see it now so clearly. You have the brightest soul I've ever seen."

"Maybe you're just going soul-blind," he grumped

Nicole coughed up blood. "You are the right one to entrust, and you will know when the time is right to pass it to Alison."

"You can't—"

James stopped as a black mist began to rise from Nicole's body, which slowly grew lighter and less substantial as the mist continued to rise. He held onto what he could for a good minute, until there was nothing left of the woman except a torn and bloody hospital gown.

The black mist slowly floated into the sky. From afar a person could easily mistake it for the plume of smoke from the burning house. Up close, even though it no longer had a human shape, James would swear ever after that he could see Nicole's face in it.

Shay walked over and touched his arm. "Brownstone, let's get the fuck out of here. We've done what we can, and at least everyone involved has been punished. Sometimes vengeance is all you can achieve."

James nodded slowly, still staring after the black mist as it rose to the heavens.

22

The next morning, James and Shay stood in front of the Anderson home.

"You sure about this, Brownstone?" Shay said. "Not too late. We can let him skitter away."

"Very sure. If you don't want to be involved, you can walk away now. I won't hold it against you. This has been my business from the beginning."

She gave him a quick shake of her head. "After everything I saw and heard yesterday, I can't walk away either."

"I gave him a chance to get away. He should have taken it." James knocked on the door. "Now his sins are gonna catch up with him."

The door opened. Walt Anderson stood on the other side, his face and nose purple and black. His mouth twitched for a moment, revealing a wired jaw.

His eyes widened, and the man backpedaled so fast he tripped over a coffee table in the living room, sprawling onto his couch. He righted himself and threw his hands up in front of him as if they could somehow stop the pair from coming into his home.

Good. Be afraid, you piece of crap.

"Hope you don't mind that I stopped by," James began, walking into the house. "I just figured it'd be great to catch up with an old friend."

Shay followed the bounty hunter in and closed the door.

"I...couldn't leave right away," Walt protested, his voice muffled and indistinct because of his jaw. "You hurt me too badly. I had to go to the hospital. I'll leave today. I promise."

James chuckled. "You can travel with a broken jaw. It doesn't matter." He strolled deeper into the house until he stood in front of the coffee table. "Know where we were yesterday?"

"I don't know. *I* was getting my jaw wired shut and pulling money out of savings. What difference does it make? You made your point before. I'm not gonna stay in L.A."

Shay leaned against the door and crossed her arms. "This ought to be fun. This little douche still thinks he gets to be pissy. Newsflash, asshole: garbage like you gets no pity."

James nodded toward Shay. "She makes a good point."

Walt groaned and pinched the bridge of his nose. "What do you want from me?"

"Just want you to listen to a little story."

"A story?"

"Yeah, about how I paid a little visit to your Harriken friends," James said. "You can read about it in the papers.

Big bloodbath. Real unfortunate. Lots of tears and bullets spent."

"T-that was you? They said...people were burned alive and blown apart by magic."

The bounty hunter managed to chuckle. "That part actually *wasn't* me."

A look of relief spread over Walt's face.

"That was Nicole," James told him.

The other man paled. He shuddered, and for a second James thoought Walt might vomit.

"N-Nicole?"

"Yep. After we freed your wife from the torture room in the basement, she decided to give a little demonstration of her power. It didn't end well for the guys who pissed her off."

Sweat beaded on Walt's forehead. "I-I'll make it up to her. Somehow."

"Too late, asshole," James said through clenched teeth. "She's dead."

The traitorous husband let out a sigh of relief. "Then it's over. It's all over."

"Oh, no, it's not over." The bounty hunter shook his head. "Because not everyone involved in this bullshit received their proper punishment. The Harriken are mostly dead, so they got what was coming to them. Funny thing is, they would have never known about Nicole if a certain asshole hadn't told them."

Walt swallowed, and his lip quivered. "We've all made mistakes. You telling me you've never done something you've regretted? I know the kind of man you are. You've got a lot more blood on your hands than I do."

James looked over at Shay, and she faked gagging. The bounty hunter stepped forward and ax-kicked the coffee table, snapping it in half. Walt yelped, then winced.

"Regretted?" James growled. "You're right, I've got enough blood on my hands to fill a river. My whole life is nothing but regrets, you piece of shit, but you know what I *wouldn't* do? Sell my wife and child to gangsters." He stomped through the debris of the table to loom over the cowering man. "You know what they did to try and get that wish out of her, don't you, Walt?"

The other man waved his hands in front of himself. "Y-you don't understand. She's not even human. You said it yourself…she used magic to kill people in twisted ways. She's practically a demon."

"So it's so much better for your Harriken buddies to stab and shoot people to death?"

"She lied to me." Walt shook his head. "From the beginning, she lied to me."

"I'm thinking that, considering what happened, she should have stuck with that plan."

Somehow the asshole managed to work up enough courage to try to sneer, but then he winced again. "You should be on my side, right? You're human. She *wasn't* human. From the very beginning she was laughing at me, pretending to be human and not some magical freak from Oriceran."

"If you're pissed about your wife lying to you, you get a divorce." James yanked Walt up by his collar. "What you *don't* do is turn her over to psychopathic criminals who will spend days torturing her to get her to give up something that doesn't belong to them. Don't you agree, Mr. Anderson?"

"That wish belongs to me!" Walt tried to shout. "She was *my* wife. She swore to honor and cherish me, and then that inhuman bitch lied to me and hid—"

James threw him against a wall. Not hard. Well, not hard by his standards. Walt cried out as he smashed against the wall, groaning and holding his arm.

"Wrong fucking answer, douchebag. Very wrong fucking answer." The bounty hunter punted half the broken table into the wall next to Walt and splinters shot through the air. "She suffered torture and intense pain to protect something she planned to give to your daughter. Who gives a fuck if you didn't get it?"

Shay pulled out her gun. "The only thing worse than a shitty husband is a shitty father, and you're two for two. Congrats, Walt."

"No, please," he said, his hands up. "I deserve a second chance. If she had been human, none of this would have happened. It's not my fault. She lied to me. You should be taking my side. We have to maintain the purity of our planet. They'll come here with all their weird magic and freaky races, and it won't even be Earth anymore."

"Keep talking, asshole." James reached into his pocket, took out some latex gloves, and slipped them on. After that, he pulled a folded-up piece of paper out of his pocket. He tossed it in front of Walt.

"What's this?"

"Cops showed up in force yesterday at the old Belmont House resort, which just happened to be a major Harriken base. The place had mostly burned down," James shot a meaningful glance at Shay, who grinned in response, "except for the basement. Cement doesn't burn like wood. Big surprise. They found this torture cell down there, with all sorts of blood and evidence for forensics." James leaned forward. "That paper right there is your little confession, all typed out, where you admit that you sent your wife to be tortured by the Harriken and how you feel guilty for her death."

Walt shook his head. "I won't sign it. I didn't kill her, and I didn't want her dead. I just wanted the damned wish. She was the one who was being stubborn."

"You fucking turned her over to criminals to be tortured to death, you motherfucking piece of shit!" James roared. "Don't even try and pretend you're not responsible for what happened to her."

The other man whimpered.

James took a deep breath. "Anyway. It doesn't matter, because that confession talks about your connections with the Harriken. I talked with your daughter, you know. She overheard you talking to some Takahashi asshole. The police will pull the phone records and put two and two together. Then they'll know you were behind your wife's disappearance."

Confusion replaced the fear on Walt's face. "I… What? I don't understand. You're going to turn me over to the police?" He licked his lips, some of the tension visibly leaving his body. "Sure, yeah. Okay, I'll sign it then. Turn me over to the police."

James looked at Shay, and she rolled her eyes.

"No, you stupid moron," the bounty hunter said. "We're not going to turn you over to the police."

"You aren't? But I said I'd sign it."

James snorted. "No, you're gonna die here in the next few minutes. I just wanted you to know that when the police investigate they are going to realize you sold your wife out to the Harriken, so as far as anyone who will know, you were a worthless piece of shit whose death will be celebrated. Maybe if you get real lucky, your name will become famous and end up as a common saying."

Shay laughed. "Like, 'My boyfriend's such a Walt Anderson.'"

James grinned. "Exactly."

Walt stared at James, disbelief on his face. "No, no, no. You're a *bounty hunter*. Can't you make some money off me or something? Take me to the police. We can go right now."

"I have a wish, Walt," James intoned. "And that wish is for you to be dead." He pulled his gun out and aimed it at Alison's father. "Say hello to the Devil for me. Let him know my arrival time's still up in the air." He squeezed the trigger, and a single shot rang out.

Walt fell over, a bullet hole in his head and his brains splattered behind him on the wall.

Shay walked over and put a single shot into his heart.

The bounty hunter and the tomb raider holstered their weapons and walked to the door.

"This still may bring heat on you, Brownstone," Shay reminded him, opening the door. "The cops might figure out it was you."

"Don't care. He had it coming, and I made a promise."

The F-350 pulled into the church's parking lot.

James looked at Shay, who was in the passenger seat. "You could always come in and unburden your soul. I'm sure the priests would love a new soul to save."

"They don't have enough priests in the world to take care of my soul." She shook her head. "Go do your thing. I'll wait here. I think I'd spontaneously combust if I went into one of those places."

James chuckled. "Fair enough."

He hurried out of the truck and into the church. The nave lay empty, so he hurried directly to the confessional.

A few moments passed before he heard Father McCartney sit on the other side and slide the grate open.

"Bless me father, for I have sinned," James intoned.

"I don't even know if we should repeat this process," said the priest, weariness in his voice. "You already pre-confessed to what you were planning to do, so it seems a bit much to go over it again."

James grunted. "Pre-confessed?"

"Aren't you here to talk about the Belmont House? I presume that bloodbath was your handiwork."

It took all James' self-control not to laugh. "Not entirely. My handiwork, that is."

"Not entirely?" Father McCartney let out a quiet groan. "You're making new friends, then? Violent friends?"

"Yes. A friend helped me, and a woman who was tortured there also got her revenge. She was already dying, but she had powerful magical abilities."

Father McCartney sighed. "Tortured? May the Lord have mercy on her soul. So much blood, James. This was different than your bounty work. This—"

"It's over, Father. The woman who was tortured was at the center of it—all of it. She wasn't human. She was a powerful princess from Oriceran. She'd taken a human husband, and was just trying to live a peaceful life."

"Trying?"

James took several breaths. Rage flowed into him, but he wouldn't let it spill out on holy ground. "I don't understand it all, Father. Her people granted her a wish."

"A wish? As in, a miracle?"

"Yes, something like that."

"And what did she use it for?"

"Nothing. She wanted to give it to her daughter, but her human husband realized what she was and wanted the wish. That was why he set her up and sold her to the Harriken. Now, her daughter... That poor girl is without her mother."

"Greed is seductive, James. It's easy to justify in people's minds, compared to a lot of other sinful motivations. But as you said, the mother is dead. Then it's all over. The wish is gone."

The bounty hunter considered lying. Father McCartney knowing about the wish could potentially put him in danger, but even if James was no longer confessing his sins, he was still talking to his confessor in a church and he couldn't bring himself to stain the ritual space with a lie. He decided to split the difference and leave out some information.

"The wish is gone from the mom," he said quietly. "It was...reassigned."

"Reassigned?"

"It's waiting for her daughter now."

Father McCartney took a deep breath. "The girl you wanted me to take care of?"

"Yes, but I have an idea. You'll probably think I lost my dam— That I've come up with better ideas, but it's the only thing I could think of."

James could hear the priest shift in his seat.

"What, James?"

"I'm not a good man, Father, and my hands are stained with so much blood. You of all people know that, but I can use my strength in a good way by protecting that girl until she gets her wish."

"Penance can take many forms. In all the chaos and change that Oriceran has brought to our world, we should not doubt that our Lord has a plan for Earth and each of us. I believe this girl is part of his plan for you, James. Part of your penance for your sins."

James swallowed. "I'll do my best."

"I know you will. Go with God, James." Father McCartney slid the grate closed.

James turned to leave, but the grate slid back open.

"James?"

"Yeah?"

"What's the girl's wish?" the priest asked.

James chuckled. "God only knows."

FINIS

Continue the story

Brownstone now has a young lady to support, what is he going to do?

He requests a special Oriceran artifact the Professor is willing to trade, for a *price*.

Click here to read Rejected By Heaven, book two in the Unbelievable Mr. Brownstone series.

First, let me say THANK YOU for not only reading this story, but going all the way through to the back here, as well!

I often write these author notes thinking, "Well, everyone knows me, so I'll just keep writing as if they have read the hundred and some-odd *other* author notes..."

I'm going to assume you don't know much about me, and this book is your first Michael Anderle story.

Two and a half years ago, I was just a guy who loved to read. So much that I read over fifty books a year for years and years and... Let's just say I'm pretty old and leave it there, okay?

Like so many readers, I wanted to write as well and Amazon offered me the chance to be an indie author where I could publish my stories myself.

So I did.

Due to amazing fans, I was allowed the chance to write —and write more and more. Now, I've got over thirty of my own books, plus four under a pen name (Michael Todd) and over a hundred collaboration books.

I am learning all the time. One of the things that I heard in late 2016 was about what happens when your series ends and you have to start another one from scratch.

It seems dangerous! I was going to be finishing my Kurtherian Gambit series in just a year, and what was I going to do then? Would fans read anything else by me? Would I go to the dusty Author Corral up in the sky?

I was a little worried, I'll admit.

The second issue I was having at this time revolved around character burn-out and "bright shiny ideas..." As an author, I usually don't lack ideas.

This is true for most authors.

The difference between me and a lot of authors is that I am much older, and I know as a reader I don't WANT my author to start placing a bunch of other stories and series and stuff when he is writing the main story I found him/her writing.

I had at least ten (10) books to go on the Kurtherian Gambit—and I wasn't going to stop that to create something new—but I didn't want to have nothing waiting for me when I finished TKG and was allowed a bit of time to go play with something else.

So, I called up Martha Carr and asked her if she wanted to do a series together (*The Leira Chronicles*).

I said "series," she heard "Universe," and the Oriceran Universe was born. (There are WHOLE other stories we can talk about related to how the Universe grew with other amazing authors such as SM Boyce, Sarah Noffke, Abby

Lynn Knorr, and Flint Maxwell – check out their stories as well!)

However, my first call to Martha was almost a year ago.

The first book in the Universe came out July 31st, 2017 and I had months and months and books and books to go before I was able to play in this new Universe.

Now you have read the first book in my new series. The first chapter was written about a year ago, but it took a lot of time to get the rest of these stories going.

When I first started writing, I wasn't sure how well I would do with a male protagonist. It took me some time to mature as an author to create the kind of male protagonists I would want to read. It started with John Grimes in *Queen Bitch* (and the whole series), and that character would influence James Brownstone.

He's a kick-ass guy who isn't afraid to care about others.

The difference is that with James Brownstone, I wanted to have a guy who has a few problems.

John Grimes is damned good-looking. Brownstone has a face only a half-blind dog could love… Or females who can see his inner core, not his external looks.

He isn't a well-heeled university catch. He isn't a billionaire or a SEAL or anything like that, for the romance types. He's a bounty hunter, and he has a few secrets. He doesn't mistreat women, but he doesn't understand them, nor will he pander to them or their crazy notions (the lush witch, as an example, or Shay's demands that he come out of the closet.)

A lot of critics will talk about having a character who needs to grow; to slowly gain their powers. However, I suggest that growing in ass-kicking skill is not the only way to engage a character arc.

I suggest you might have a good guy, who likes life simple. Then, throw in two females, one a multi-racial teenager whose mom comes from another world, and an adult female ex-killer trying to go straight who has a few hangups of her own.

Life just keeps getting more and more complicated for James Brownstone, having neither mother nor father in his life, who is trying his *best* to be a good father figure for a young girl.

A role life NEVER set him up to know anything about.

Jessie Rae's

When I create stories, I start with the characters…for the most part. I want at least two (my preference is three) characters where I know just enough about them that I can see where the character conflict occurs.

Hopefully, with a lot of opportunity for fun.

For Brownstone, I did something VERY straightforward and very male in my neck of the woods (I'm Texan by birth)—the man loves his barbeque.

He eats barbeque…and sleeps it, and breathes in the nectar of the smoke every chance he gets. If he isn't kicking ass, he is thinking about barbeque, or eating it.

The problem isn't that I don't know anything about barbeque; far from it. Rather, I know enough that I absolutely know that *I don't know enough!*

So, what's an author to do? GET HELP!

Here in Vegas, where we are domiciling for now, the

only barbeque places I knew were in Casinos. That wasn't the type of knowledge I wanted. I wanted someone who would know barbeque like James did. Someone he could chat with, and get down and discuss the fine nuances of different styles.

I happened to get on Yelp one morning when I was overwhelmed by a NEED to eat some barbeque. After looking at the different reviews, I chose to check out Jessie Rae's across the 15 from Mandalay Bay.

Now, I live on the Strip not that far from Mandalay Bay, so It was easy enough for me to head south and then jump across the freeway to find the place.

It's small. In fact, we couldn't hold an event there for more than thirty people, I'd bet ya. They have their barbeque pits out back, not inside running on gas like many of the chain locations.

I was working at the restaurant—working out the beats for this book—and I worked up the courage to ask the guy (young guy) who seemed to be the owner if he would consider helping me by becoming a consultant on this book.

Fortunately Mike LOVES books, and thought being included in one in whatever form or fashion I contrived would be fantastic!

It was a LOT of weeks between that first meeting and now when we are about to publish the book I spoke to him about so long ago.

I have gone back to Jessie Rae's quite a few times (the food is damned good, and the #GodSauce is fantastic...but I digress), and I saw Mike maybe every other trip. He was doing the delivery driving one time, taking orders another, back in the kitchen on a third trip, and so on. I've met his mom working there, and I think I saw/met his wife, but I'm not positive (she is the "Jessie Rae" the place is named after.)

Personally, I LOVE to put real people into my stories, and places that fans, if they want to, can visit. Now, I learned a lot from things I did in The Kurtherian Gambit and I'm amping up the coolness factor (for me, anyway) by inviting Mike to provide his own form of Author Notes.

Because, who doesn't want to know about barbeque?

So, I'll end by saying *THANK YOU* so freaking much for reading Brownstone. I hope you join us for the second book, *Rejected by Heaven,* which is coming out in just two (2) weeks. Continue turning the pages here to see what Mike has to say about his story…and barbeque.

Ad Aeternitatem,

Michael Anderle

BBQ NOTES - MIKE ROSS

WRITTEN APRIL 5, 2018

Michael Anderle here. I know you will find this difficult to believe, but Mike Ross of Jessie Rae's BBQ thinks of himself more as a man of meat and less a man of the *pen*.

(Or typewriter, word processor...you get the idea.)

So I sent him a few questions, and here are his answers to three of them. (I'll get that recipe out of him by the next book...I hope. Getting recipes for anything out of cooks can be such a challenge. I'm not asking for a personal recipe they USE in the restaurant, just one that he thinks is good.)

Check in at the back of the next Brownstone book, *Rejected by Heaven,* to see if I'm successful!

QUESTIONS:

Michael: *what are your thoughts about your (Jessie Rae's) involvement in* The Unbelievable Mr. Brownstone *series?*

Mike R: I am humbled to be a part of something that will honestly go down in history. Being a part of a book/novel/series is something one dreams about if you

love books and reading. And I (well, Jessie Rae's BBQ) has been lucky enough to be chosen to live that dream.

Michael: *I know from talking with your mom—I was there for lunch and she was minding the store—that she encouraged a love of books, and you took that up from a pretty early age. However, starting a business is hard, tough, and takes a lot of hours. How do you get your fix in now?*

Mike R: "Books on tape" is one of the *greatest* inventions. While I'm a very busy guy, I STILL love books, and I just don't get enough...*bathroom* time like I did in the past (Ha-ha).

Being able to just press Play and pop the headphones on while smoking our meats or driving to our next catering event has been awesome!

Between my wife and me we have three Audible accounts, so we can *always* have the latest book that month!

Michael: *Why did you name it after your wife, and is her name Jessie Rae?*

Mike R: My wife's full name is "Jessica Rae," "Jessie Rae" for short. She is the *backbone* of the business, and why I'm involved in BBQ in the first place.

She supported my "silly barbeque hobby" from day one.

She bought me my first smoker, and was also my partner in the creation of our award-winning barbeque sauce.

So after our first competition, where we placed well in some meat categories and won second place for Best BBQ Sauce in Nevada, I got the nerve to smoke for some friends and family and they loved it.

A short time after this, a friend of the family loaned us some startup money and we found the little dive we are in now, (it has doubled in size since we got it), and from there business just took off!

Two years later, we are still going strong. We're in a book, for crying out loud! I would have to say we've made it!

Michael again... Okay, that's all I could get out of Mike Ross for this book. However, I'm going to SACRIFICE myself by taking my body back to Jessie Rae's and eating barbeque just so I can corner Mike about the recipe for the next book.

If I fail on the first attempt, I shall go BACK for another lunch and do it all again.

Never let it be said that I'm not willing to eat the extra mile for my fans!

RECIPES FROM THE FANS

WRITTEN APRIL 5, 2018

So, *I've* got to pin down Mike Ross next time I eat at Jessie Rae's for a recipe (I know, it's my *sacrifice.*)

HOWEVER, in my moment of need, the FANS CAME THROUGH!

Fortunately, just enough of you did the job. So, I'm adding every recipe that didn't link somewhere (I can't add those) that I found before I finished this document and sent it to Stephen Campbell (Zen Master Walking™).

THANK YOU ALL!

Michael Anderle

Morgan Walczak (Permission Granted!)

My family uses this on pork butts, but whatever we have left we freeze for later.

Ready? *(Ma said its ok to share this family secret!)*
- 4 cups Dr Pepper
- 4 cups ketchup
- 4 cups apple cider vinegar
- 2 oz black pepper
- 6 oz onion powder
- 4 oz garlic powder
- 4 oz cayenne pepper
- 4 cups honey
- 2 cups Worcestershire Sauce
- 1/2 cup corn starch for thickness

Enjoy. (It is yummy as hell!)

Mix it all except cornstarch and simmer for thirty minutes. Add cornstarch mixed with a little water and cook until thickened.

Mary Gustafson (BBQ Country Style Pork Ribs – Slow Cooked!)

My mom used to make this when short ribs were cheap and a good solution when feeding six hungry teenagers. It is the whole recipe, not just the sauce. Hope it fits here (it does!)

Feeds 6 to 8
- 5 Pounds country style pork ribs
- 3 Tbl BBQ rub – Pick your favorite (optional)
- 1 cup Catsup

1 cup Cider vinegar
3 Tbl Worcestershire sauce
2 Tbl Brown Sugar
2 Cloves garlic - minced
¼ tsp hot pepper sauce

Water as needed – (½ cup generally.)

Rub the ribs with the rub. Grill over hot coals for 4-5 minutes per side. (Or broil them for a few minutes per side.)

Place ribs in a large slow cooker, roaster or covered roasting pan. Combine other ingredients (except water) and pour over the ribs.

Cook at about 275 degrees for 4-5 hours. Add a little water if needed. Rotate the ribs every couple of hours to ensure that they cook evenly.

You can serve this a couple of different ways.

First, merely place the ribs on a platter. Pour the sauce into a separator and let the grease rise to the top. Pour off the grease and serve the sauce with the ribs.

Alternately, let the ribs cool a bit and then pick out the meat, discarding the fat and bones. You may want to pull the meat apart with a couple of forks. Again separate the sauce and pour over the meat. Serve with buns.

You can also make this ahead, cool it overnight in the refrigerator and then reheat it to serve on buns.

It keeps well and reheats well, especially if it's been covered in sauce.

This is great to do when country style pork ribs are on sale. You can use either the bone in or boneless. I prefer the flavor of the bone in.

Karl Fitchey (BEER!)
    1 tablespoon butter
    1 cup finely diced red onion
    ½ cup dark beer*
    1/4 teaspoon kosher salt
    3 garlic cloves, minced
    1 jalapeño, seeded and finely diced
    1 teaspoon smoked paprika
    1/4 teaspoon cayenne pepper
    2 cups ketchup
    3 tablespoons dark brown sugar
    2 tablespoons soy sauce
    2 tablespoons Worcestershire sauce
    1 tablespoon apple cider vinegar
    2 tablespoons lemon juice

1. In a medium saucepan, melt the butter over medium-low heat. Add the onion, beer, and salt, stir, cover, and cook gently for fifteen minutes, watching carefully and stirring every few minutes so the onion doesn't stick to the

pan. Add the remaining ingredients, stir, and bring to a simmer. Let the sauce simmer away for thirty minutes, stirring every so often.

2. Using an immersion blender, puree the sauce directly in the pot until smooth. (Alternatively, carefully transfer the sauce to a regular blender and puree until smooth. Be careful when blending hot liquids.)

3. Transfer to a jar, let cool completely, and store in the fridge overnight to allow the flavors to develop.

The BBQ sauce will keep in an airtight container in the fridge for about two weeks.

*Use VERY DARK beer - (*I use Mississippi Mud.*)

Carol Lynn Lewis Blankenship (A Father's Love)

One of my fav memories of my Step-father (who I don't consider step) was of him making homemade BBQ Sauce.

He would get in the kitchen and pull out a Bottle of Ketchup (that evil stuff I don't like but is a staple in his BBQ sauce, which I love)
   1 onion chopped up fine,
   1 clove of garlic minced,
   1/2 cup of Brown sugar,
   about 1/4th cup of Mustard,
   Little Salt and pepper.

He would sauté the onions in oil and drain. Pour in the ketchup (he always de-glazed the pan with the Ketchup, added the mustard salt and pepper and then simmer. The flavor is sweet and tangy. He would add more mustard occasionally.

I used to cry every time he tried to make it as his Alzheimer's got worse.

Mom always tried to make it his way but never got the hang of it (but then again this is the same woman who made HOCKEY pucks for Biscuits! As a kid we literately went outside and used them like pucks one time.)

Nicole Emens (Nana's Sauce)

This is the one my Nana taught me. She came to the U.S from Hungary in the early 1900's. She taught me how to cook, and boy oh boy, could *she* cook!

She came through Ellis island and her name is on the wall there. I have the first dollar she ever made here in the USA, an 1892 Morgan. She worked in the sweat shops in NYC until they were shut down.

She was an amazing woman!
    4 TBS olive oil
    3/4 cup onion chopped fine,
    4 cloves garlic chopped fine
    30 oz tomato sauce
    1 cup catsup

4 TBS cider vinegar

4 TBS lemon juice

4 TBS sweet vermouth

1/2 cup dark brown sugar

4 TBS chili powder

2 TSP Paprika

2 TSP dry mustard powder

1/4 black pepper

Sautee onions in oil until translucent than add garlic, sauté until brown, add rest of ingredients and bring to a simmer, let it simmer for 30 min.

Now it's ready to be placed in jars

Kathleen Fettig's Barbeque Sauce

Here is my own recipe for bbq sauce. I love this in a crock pot with country ribs or added to a cowboy beans recipe.

1 pint ketchup - Hunts

1/3 cup brown sugar

1/2 cup chopped onion

2 TBL mustard (prepared)

1/3 cup molasses

1/3 cup water

2 TBL vinegar

If using on meat being grilled, make the recipe and simmer it for half an hour to blend all the flavors before using. I usually use this in a crock pot.

Tim Bischoff's Sweet/Spicy Kentucky Bourbon BBQ Sauce

All ingredients should be organic or best quality

About 1 half gallon = final result

3 ½ cups of Tomato Paste

3 ½ cups of Apple Cider Vinegar

1 cup of Evan Williams Bourbon (preferably Even Williams 1783 aged 10 years, Black label will do)

1 cup of Brown Sugar

1 cup of White Cane Sugar

1 cup of Molasses

2.5 oz of Worcestershire sauce

1 ½ tbsp of paprika

2 ½ tsp of fresh ground pepper

2 ½ tsp of fine kosher salt

2 ½ tsp of Franks Red Hot sauce

½ tsp of chipotle powder

¼ stick of butter

1 sweet onion finely minced (sautéed in the butter)

2 cloves of Garlic finely minced (sautéed in the butter)

Up to 1 bottle of KY Bourbon Barrel Ale (if not available in your area, another beer or water can be used)

1. Sautee the onion and garlic in a soup pot (large enough so mixing is easy)

2. Next add other ingredients (except water) slowly into the pan mixing well

3. Next add 1 cup of the water whisking well.

4. Simmer slowly for about an hour and half

Note: Franks Red Hot Sauce, Chipotle Powder can be adjusted if you like your sauce less spicy (try making a smaller batch to find your own desired taste)

Tim Bischoff's KY Dry Rub

(Optional as additional flavor as heavy or light as desired)
- 3 tablespoons Bourbon-infused Salt (kosher salt will work as a substitute)
- 3 tablespoons chili powder
- 3 tablespoons paprika
- 2 tablespoons fresh ground black pepper
- 2 tablespoons brown sugar
- 2 tablespoons dry mustard
- 1 tablespoon chipotle powder
- 1 tablespoon garlic powder

Smoking needs

A good quality smoker to maintain temperature around 200 degrees

Staves from used bourbon barrels cut into small pieces to produce a unique smoke flavor.

Other woods can be used depending on a person's taste such as Hickory, Mesquite, Apple. Not just any wood can be used to produce a quality product.

Baste meats about every thirty minutes.

Cooking time will vary depending on the type and thickness of the meat, but this is a long slow process.

Brandon Leask (Humorous Mention)

The hardest part about bbq sauce is braving the <redacted> ppl on the way to the store to buy me some *Sweet Baby Rays.*

Have you read The Kurtherian Gambit, from Michael Anderle?

Available at Amazon

Glow (1) Shimmer (2) Ember (3) Nightfall (4)

Evacuation (01) - Retaliation (02) - Revelations (03) - Redemption (04)

RECLAIMING HONOR
with Justin Sloan

Justice Is Calling (01) - Claimed By Honor (02) - Judgement Has Fallen (03) - Angel of Reckoning (04) - Born Into Flames (05) - Defending The Lost (06) - Saved By Valor (07) - Return of Victory (08)

THE ETHERIC ACADEMY
with TS Paul

ALPHA CLASS (01) - ALPHA CLASS: Engineering (02)
with N.D. Roberts

Discovery (03)

TERRY HENRY "TH" WALTON CHRONICLES
with Craig Martelle

Nomad Found (01) - Nomad Redeemed (02) - Nomad Unleashed (03) - Nomad Supreme (04) - Nomad's Fury (05) - Nomad's Justice (06) - Nomad Avenged (07) - Nomad Mortis (08) - Nomad's Force (09) - Nomad's Galaxy (10)

TRIALS AND TRIBULATIONS
with Natalie Grey

Risk Be Damned (01) - Damned to Hell (02)

~THE AGE OF MAGIC~

THE RISE OF MAGIC

Bitch's Night Out: Frank Kurns Stories of the UnknownWorld 02 (9.5)

with Natalie Grey

Bellatrix: Frank Kurns Stories of the Unknownworld 03 (13.25)

Challenges: Frank Kurns Stories of the Unknownworld 04

AudioBooks

Available at Audible.com and iTunes

CLICK HERE TO SEE ALL LMBPN BOOKS ON AUDIBLE

CONNECT WITH MICHAEL ANDERLE

Michael Anderle Social
Website:
http://kurtherianbooks.com/

Email List:
http://kurtherianbooks.com/email-list/

Facebook Here:
https://www.facebook.com/OriceranUniverse/
https://www.facebook.com/TheKurtherianGambitBooks/

Made in the USA
Monee, IL
03 July 2022